## "We're definitely not friends."

"Oh, I don't know." Dane's voice slid low and deep, sending shivers down her spine—shivers of heat that were reflected in the blue of his eyes when he looked at her. "You seemed to like me well enough last night."

Stacey swallowed. "I don't..."

"Don't remember?" His smile spoke of intimate secrets and stole her breath. "I'm not surprised. You were pretty much out of it when you grabbed me."

"When *I* grabbed *you?*"

"Don't worry." His smile widened. "I didn't mind at all. In fact, you can feel free to grab me and kiss me again—"

"*Kiss* you?" Had she done that? Had she actually *done* that?

"—any time you want."

"When pigs fly."

Dear Reader,

June is busting out all over with this month's exciting lineup!

First up is Annette Broadrick's *But Not For Me*. We asked Annette what kinds of stories she loved, and she admitted that a heroine in love with her boss has always been one of her favorites. In this romance, a reserved administrative assistant falls for her sexy boss, but leaves her position when she receives threatening letters. Well, this boss has another way to keep his beautiful assistant by his side—marry her right away!

*Royal Protocol* by Christine Flynn is the next installment of the CROWN AND GLORY series. Here, a lovely lady-in-waiting teaches an admiral a thing or two about chemistry. Together, they try to rescue royalty, but end up rescuing each other. And you can never get enough of Susan Mallery's DESERT ROGUES series. In *The Prince & the Pregnant Princess,* a headstrong woman finds out she's pregnant with a seductive sheik's child. How long will it take before she succumbs to his charms and his promise of happily ever after?

In *The Last Wilder,* the fiery conclusion of Janis Reams Hudson's WILDERS OF WYATT COUNTY, a willful heroine on a secret quest winds up in a small town and locks horns with the handsome local sheriff. Cheryl St.John's *Nick All Night* tells the story of a down-on-her-luck woman who returns home and gets a second chance at love with her very distracting next-door neighbor. In Elizabeth Harbison's *Drive Me Wild,* a schoolbus-driving mom struggles to make ends meet, but finds happiness with a former flame who just happens to be her employer!

It's time to enjoy those lazy days of summer. So, grab a seat by the pool and don't forget to bring your stack of emotional tales of love, life and family from Silhouette Special Edition!

Sincerely,

Karen Taylor Richman
Senior Editor

Please address questions and book requests to:
Silhouette Reader Service
U.S.: 3010 Walden Ave., P.O. Box 1325, Buffalo, NY 14269
Canadian: P.O. Box 609, Fort Erie, Ont. L2A 5X3

# The Last Wilder

## JANIS REAMS HUDSON

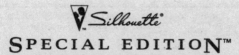

**SPECIAL EDITION**™

Published by Silhouette Books

America's Publisher of Contemporary Romance

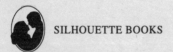 SILHOUETTE BOOKS

ISBN 0-373-24474-6

THE LAST WILDER

Copyright © 2002 by Janis Reams Hudson

This edition published by arrangement with Harlequin Books S.A.

® and TM are trademarks of Harlequin Books S.A., used under license.
Trademarks indicated with ® are registered in the United States Patent
and Trademark Office, the Canadian Trade Marks Office and in other
countries.

Visit Silhouette at www.eHarlequin.com

**Printed in U.S.A.**

**Books by Janis Reams Hudson**

**Silhouette Special Edition**

*Resist Me If You Can* #1037
*The Mother of His Son* #1095
*His Daughter's Laughter* #1105
*Until You* #1210
*\*Their Other Mother* #1267
*\*The Price of Honor* #1332
*\*A Child on the Way* #1349
*\*Daughter on His Doorstep* #1434
*\*The Last Wilder* #1474

\*Wilders of Wyatt County

## JANIS REAMS HUDSON

was born in California, grew up in Colorado, lived in Texas for a few years and now calls central Oklahoma home. She is the author of more than twenty-five novels, both contemporary and historical romances. Her books have appeared on the Waldenbooks, B. Dalton and Bookrack bestseller lists and earned numerous awards, including the National Readers' Choice Award and Reviewer's Choice awards from *Romantic Times*. She is a three-time finalist for the coveted RITA® Award from Romance Writers of America and is a past president of RWA.

# THE WILDERS

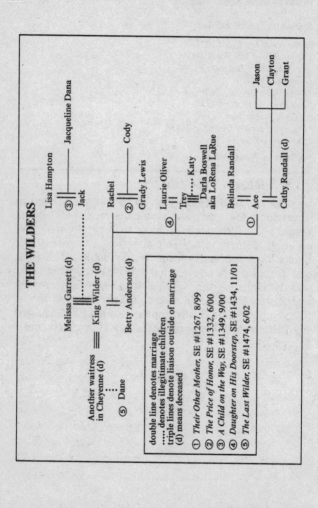

Another waitress in Cheyenne (d) ≡ King Wilder (d) = Melissa Garrett (d)

⑤ Dane

Lisa Hampton
③ Jack = Jacqueline Dana

Betty Anderson (d)

Rachel — Cody
② Grady Lewis

Laurie Oliver
④ Trey ⋮ Katy
    Darla Boswell
    aka LoRena LaRue

Belinda Randall
① Ace = Cathy Randall (d)

Jason
Clayton
Grant

---

double line denotes marriage
.... denotes illegitimate children
triple lines denote liaison outside of marriage
(d) means deceased

① *Their Other Mother*, SE #1267, 8/99
② *The Price of Honor*, SE #1332, 6/00
③ *A Child on the Way*, SE #1349, 9/00
④ *Daughter on His Doorstep*, SE #1434, 11/01
⑤ *The Last Wilder*, SE #1474, 6/02

## Chapter One

Wyatt County Sheriff Dane Powell stood in the shadow of a truck-sized boulder at the edge of the ravine and watched the beam of a flashlight bob and weave its way down the rise a hundred yards away, where no flashlight—no person—should be at two o'clock this cold Saturday morning.

He wouldn't have noticed that the Wilders had a trespasser on the back side of their Flying Ace ranch if he hadn't spotted the snazzy red sports car with no tag, half-concealed in the bushes beside the road. He might not have noticed the car if he hadn't been specifically looking for anything out of the ordinary.

In fact, he wouldn't have been on patrol at all at this time of night but for the cattle rustlers that had moved their operation into his county a few weeks ago.

He watched the spot of light bob its way down the

rise. As bright as the moon was, a flashlight was only barely necessary. Dane could just make out the figure of a person, but couldn't tell anything about him other than that he was bundled up in a heavy coat against the frigid night. Nobody said cattle rustlers had to be stupid.

This might not be one of the rustlers. Dane had to remind himself of that. But what else anybody would be doing out here at this time of night, he couldn't imagine. At the least, the guy was a trespasser.

The suspect hit level ground, then, after a few yards, started carefully down into the ravine. There was no other way to get to the road. Moonlight reflected off the small cloud of dust the guy kicked up on his way down.

With the fellow out of sight and making enough noise with his grunting and cursing and kicking up rocks to cover any sound Dane might make, Dane moved in and stood ten feet back from the spot where he figured the guy would climb up out of the ravine.

It could be a woman, Dane supposed. The build was slight enough. But he couldn't imagine a woman out here at this time of night on her own. Frankly he couldn't imagine a man out here, either. Not for any legitimate reason.

The grunting and scrabbling noises from down in the ravine crept closer and closer to the rim until first a gloved hand, then a head appeared.

Dane switched on his flashlight and aimed it straight in the trespasser's face. "Evening. Nice night for a stroll."

In the space of one second, before the shriek, before the startled trespasser lost balance and tumbled back down the steep embankment in a hail of rocks and a cloud of dust, Dane could have sworn he saw an angel.

Pale gold shoulder-length hair surrounded a creamy face with high cheekbones reddened by the cold, a narrow nose and a dainty chin. Startled eyes of baby blue widened, then blinked. Her mouth flew open and formed a perfect *O*.

Then came the shriek and the backward tumble.

As far as Dane knew, angels didn't shriek. Nor did they cuss a blue streak. This was a woman. A red-blooded, fury-spitting woman. A beautiful woman, who might possibly be hurt after a fall like that.

Flashlight in hand, Dane scrambled down into the cloud of dust still hovering in the air at the bottom of the ravine. "Are you all right?"

Stacey Landers eyed the man looming over her. She didn't know which struck sharper—her anger, mistrust or outright fear.

Where had he come from? One minute she was alone in the wilderness, the next, some bozo was blinding her with his flashlight.

"Are you all right?" he asked again. Except he didn't ask; he demanded.

Oh, great, a demanding bozo. "Just dandy," she ground out.

"Here, let me help you." The man reached for her arm.

Visions of her mangled body—beaten, stabbed, strangled or perhaps shot—flashed sheer terror through Stacey's mind. She scrambled backward on her rear across the dirt and gravel, ignoring the way every sharp little rock, and some not so little, gouged into her rear. Her defenses were pitifully few: her wits, which were slightly scattered after that tumble down the embankment; and her flashlight, which had quit working during the fall and still refused to produce so much as a flicker of light no matter how many times she hit the switch.

She decided to try out the old saying and go with a good offense. "Get away from me." She hefted the flashlight and waved it before her. "I've got a flashlight, and I know how to use it."

"Yes, ma'am," he said, backing off a pace. "I can see that. I just want to help."

*So you say.* "When I need help, I'll ask for it." He didn't look like one of the men she'd hidden from earlier, but she hadn't gotten a good look at all of them as she'd hunkered down in the rocks and watched them load cattle into a huge trailer. She knew she wasn't supposed to be here, but she hadn't been able to say no to her grandmother's request for this secret errand. Now Gran was going to have a fit when she learned Stacey had been not only seen but confronted.

"Can you get up?" the man asked.

"Of course." Looming over her the way he was, he looked like a menacing giant, which did nothing for Stacey's peace of mind. "If you'll back off and quit crowding me."

He raised both hands in the air. "Backing off."

Stacey pushed herself to her feet, but when she stepped back to put more distance between herself and the stranger, pain shot upward from her right ankle to her knee. The world momentarily went black. She cried out. Her leg folded and she ended up once again on her butt in the dirt.

The man cursed and knelt beside her. "I thought

you said you were all right. What is it—your knee? Ankle?''

''Ankle.'' She hated the way her voice quivered, but at least her vision was clearing.

Placing his flashlight on the ground so that it shone on her ankle, the man reached for the hem of her jeans. ''Can you wiggle your toes?'' His hands were warm and surprisingly gentle as he felt from her shin to her foot.

''Yes,'' she answered. ''I don't think anything's broken.''

''Doesn't feel like it. You probably just twisted it,'' he offered. Then, without so much as a by-your-leave, with his flashlight in one hand, he lifted her in his arms and stood.

''Hey, wait a minute, buster,'' Stacey protested, feeling way too vulnerable cradled in his arms as if she were a child. She still had her own flashlight clutched in her fist. She hefted it toward his head in a threatening gesture. ''You better put me down right this minute.'' If there was one thing she hated, it was a take-charge, macho-jerk. ''I mean it!''

''Calm down,'' he said easily. ''You hit me with that thing and I'll have to charge you with assaulting an officer.''

Stacey paused. ''An officer of what?''

''The law. Wyatt County Sheriff Dane Powell,'' he said as he carried her. ''At your service.''

A county sheriff. Of all the rotten luck. If there was one thing she detested more than a take-charge, macho jerk, it was a take-charge, macho-jerk, gun-toting cop. ''Where are you taking me?'' she demanded.

''Out of here.''

Stacey sniffed. She hadn't asked him to carry her, but since she couldn't walk, she decided to keep her mouth shut. For the time being.

It was disgusting the way he carried her so easily, and over rough ground, all the way to the fence, without even breathing hard. And it was disquieting the way she noticed the strength and warmth—she couldn't bring herself to think the word *comfort*—of his arms.

In a neat maneuver a contortionist would have applauded, he got them both through the barbed wire fence. Parked behind her car she spotted his white SUV with a light bar across the top and a logo on the door identifying the vehicle as belonging to the Wyatt County Sheriff. She started to demand that he take her to her car but realized she would never be able to manage the clutch, brake and accelerator with only one foot.

Maybe her ankle was better, she thought with hope. Not that she thought the sheriff was going to let her drive away without explaining what she'd been doing out there on someone's ranch in the middle of the night. She should be so lucky.

With her in his arms, he started toward his vehicle.

"Oh, no, thanks," she said. "You can just take me to my car." She would have to manage. Somehow.

In the bright moonlight and the glow of his flashlight, there was no mistaking the mocking look on the sheriff's face. "I wouldn't dream of expecting an injured woman to drive off on her own. What kind of public servant would that make me?"

"A polite one, who acceded to a woman's wishes?"

"No, no." He shook his head and stopped beside his Blazer. "An irresponsible one if I didn't check out your injury more thoroughly. Here we go," he said cheerily. He opened the passenger door of his vehicle and sat her gently on the seat, sideways, with her feet hanging out the door.

It might be a fancy sport utility vehicle, but a cop car was a cop car, Stacey thought, eyeing the police radio, the shotgun standing upright and locked in place against the dash.

"Now," he said, "let's take a better look at this ankle."

She rolled her eyes. "Yes, let's."

But no matter how hard she wished it otherwise, the ankle was not better. In fact, it was visibly swollen and hurt like blue blazes when he touched it, and again when he asked her to press the bottom of her foot against his hand, which had the same effect as putting weight on it. The ankle protested viciously. There was no way she was going to be able to drive. Dammit.

And no matter how hard she wished it otherwise, beyond the pain, there was a warmth, a comfort in his touch that sneaked into her blood. And, heaven help her, a definite sizzle.

The pain must be making her delirious. The warmth was from the interior of his vehicle, not his touch. She'd been out in the cold too long, that was all. And her blood wouldn't dare heat up at the touch of a cop. Been there, done that, got the divorce papers to prove it.

"It's probably just a bad sprain," he told her. "But we'll have the doctor take a look at it, just to be safe." He gave her a slight nudge to turn her in the seat, then closed the door, sealing her inside. When he went around and climbed into the driver's seat, she started to fish her keys out of her coat pocket so she could ask him to get her purse from the trunk of her car, but thought better of the idea and kept quiet. If he opened the trunk he'd see her tag and could run a check on her, and if she had her purse, she would have identification, which he would no doubt demand to see. She kept her hand away from the pocket containing her keys. She preferred to remain anonymous, thank you very much.

He started the engine and warm air gushed from the vents. "We'll have your car brought to town later today."

"How much later?"

Instead of answering her, the sheriff picked up his radio mic and told dispatch that he was ten-eight and to let the hospital know he was bringing in a woman with a bad sprain, so they should wake up the doctor on call.

Must be a pretty small hospital, she thought, if they didn't have a doctor on duty all night.

"What's ten-eight?" she asked. She knew a few police codes, but not that one.

"It means I'm back in service. Now," he said as he backed up and pulled out onto the gravel road, "suppose you tell me your name and what you were doing out there."

Stacey didn't bat an eye. She opened her mouth and lied through her teeth. "I'm Carla Smith."

"Smith, huh?"

"That's right. There really are people named Smith."

"Okay, Carla Smith. Were you aware you were trespassing on private property?"

She gave as good an imitation of genuine surprise as she was able. "Private property? Way out here? I didn't see a house anywhere."

"That answers one question."

"What question?"

"You're not from around here. You were a ways from the house, but you were on the Flying Ace ranch. Want to tell me why?"

"I didn't realize I was on anyone's ranch. The Flying Ace? Cool name. Did somebody win it in a card game or something?"

"As a matter of fact, yes."

"You're kidding."

"I'm not. It was more than a hundred years ago, and you didn't answer my question."

"What question?"

"What," he asked again, "were you doing out there?"

It had never occurred to Stacey that she would have to explain her trek to anyone. Who would be around to see her at this time of night?

The sheriff, that's who, and now she had to come up with an explanation. She couldn't tell him the truth. Gran had made her swear not to tell a soul. So now what was she supposed to do? *Gran, what have you gotten me into?*

"I'm waiting," the sheriff said.

Stacey swallowed. "I was walking."

"Come again?"

"I was walking. It's a great night, all that moonlight, no snow yet. I thought I might find some night-blooming cactus."

Dane nearly laughed out loud. As excuses went, that was a new one on him. "Try again."

"Try what again?"

"You do that innocent thing really good with your voice, but try a better excuse. I'm not buying night-blooming cactus."

"I'm sorry to hear that," she told him. "But I've got nothing better to offer."

"Oh," he said, "I'm sure if you put your mind to it you can come up with something, Ms. Smith." And if that was her real name, Dane thought, his was Elvis.

She didn't have a comeback for him, so they rode in silence, nothing but the hum of the tires, once they hit the blacktop, and the occasional crackle on the two-way radio. It was a long drive, nearly an hour. Dane occupied his mind with the puzzle of the woman next to him, who smelled so sweet and lied so poorly. He wanted another look at her. A good one this time, to see if she really looked as angelic as he'd first thought.

Try as he might, he could think of no legitimate reason for anyone, much less a young woman—he pegged her at around twenty-five—to be traipsing around the far side of the Flying Ace in the wee hours of a Saturday morning. And the woman in question had certainly not provided him with one.

Night-blooming cactus.

If he wasn't wondering if she might have some connection to the cattle rustlers, he could be amused by that.

But he *was* wondering. A lookout? A scout?

None of the scenarios that came to mind seemed

to work. Or rather, she didn't seem to fit any of them. Maybe he didn't want her to fit.

Whatever she'd been doing out there, Dane would know before he let her go.

At the hospital Dane carried his passenger in through the emergency entrance, where a nurse met them with a wheelchair. As was the way of hospitals everywhere, the first order of business was the paperwork.

Ms. Smith, Dane noticed as she filled out the forms, had no insurance. He made a note of the social security number she wrote down, but he'd bet his next meal that it didn't belong to anyone named Carla Smith.

In the exam room a few minutes later, with her coat draped across a chair and Dr. Will Carver bending over her ankle, Dane got his first good look at his trespasser. Her jeans were snug and soft with age. Her thick sweater draped to her hips and revealed just enough of the curves beneath to entice.

Her nose wasn't red now, as it had been in his first sight of her in the beam of his flashlight, but it was still narrow, drawing his gaze to a pair of lips curved to make a man want to take a taste. Dane was a man. The strength of the wanting that seized him as he stared at her lips told him he'd obviously been neglecting his social life way too long. At best she was a trespasser. At the worst...

But she was a looker, with that dainty chin, pale blue eyes and a thick halo of light gold hair that practically whispered *Come, sink your hands in me.*

That did it. He was getting out his little black book and finding himself a date the first chance he got.

He'd definitely been alone too long when a woman's hair started speaking to him, in complete sentences.

As pretty as she was, though, his trespasser looked beat. Pain tightened the skin around her mouth, and her eyes spoke of exhaustion. He wondered how long she'd been out there walking around in the dark. And what the hell she'd been doing.

He intended to find out as soon as they left the hospital.

Will poked and prodded at his patient's foot and ankle, then had the nurse wheel her down the hall for an X-ray. She was back a few minutes later, and Will put a cold pack on her ankle while they waited. It wasn't long before the X-ray was ready.

"As I thought," Will said. "Nothing's broken."

The patient grimaced. "I guess that's good. If it hurt any worse, I'd probably embarrass myself and bawl like a baby."

"I'll give you something for the pain," Will told her. "But you'll need to stay off this foot for a few days, until the swelling goes down. Alternating twenty minutes of cold with twenty of heat will help that. You've got a pulled muscle and some torn ligaments. When the swelling goes down, you can start putting some weight on it, but don't overdo it, or you'll just tear those ligaments again and build up scar tissue that will impede the flexibility of the joint."

"As much fun as it is having a big, strong man carry me around," she said with great sarcasm as she batted her lashes at Dane, "I don't think it's going to be a convenient mode of transportation for long. When will the swelling go down?"

Will chuckled. "I'd say in a couple of days, if you stay off it."

"But driving's okay, right?" she asked.

"Only if you can do it without using this foot."

She frowned. The foot in question was her right one. "You're just full of good news."

Will held his arms out from his sides. "It could be worse. We'll fix you up with a pair of crutches before you leave, if that helps."

She shook her head and smiled sheepishly. "It will. I'm sorry. It's not your fault I've crippled myself." She placed special emphasis on the word *your* and shot Dane a look that said it was *his* fault.

Dane arched his brow and folded his arms across his chest. "I guess that's just one of the hazards of searching for night-blooming cactus."

Will scratched his head and frowned. "What?"

"Never mind," his patient said swiftly.

The only piece of business left after she familiarized herself with her new crutches was to pay for the services rendered.

Of course, the woman had no purse on her, therefore, no money.

Dane bit back a curse. "Bill my office, will you?" he asked the nurse who doubled as a clerk at this time of night.

"How kind, Sheriff." The woman with the crutches tucked beneath her arms gave him a biting grin.

"You'll pay me back," he told her tersely.

"I doubt it, seeing how this was all your fault in the first place."

Dane opened his mouth, ready to point out the obvious, that had she not been breaking the law to begin with by trespassing on private property, she wouldn't have fallen and hurt herself. But he kept silent, not wanting to air the matter in front of the all-too-curious hospital staff. He figured it must get pretty boring around the hospital in the middle of the night. He didn't want to leave them any more fuel for gossip than necessary.

He strode to the door and held it open. "After you," he said to the woman calling herself Carla Smith.

She paused in the doorway and looked at him suspiciously. "Where are we going?"

"I'll buy you a cup of coffee."

"And in exchange, you expect me to tell you the story of my life?"

"The story of your night will do for starters."

"Now why," she muttered as she crutched her way out into the cold night, "did I know he was going to say that."

Dane bit back a sudden grin and followed her.

## Chapter Two

The sign over the rear entrance of the three-story granite building read Wyatt County Courthouse.

Stacey narrowed her eyes. "Why are we here?" She turned her gaze on the sheriff, noticing, not for the first time, the strong shape of his lips.

"It's the only place in town that serves coffee at this time of night."

*Yeah, right,* Stacey thought, irritated with herself for liking the way his mouth moved when he spoke. "The courthouse serves coffee?"

"My office serves coffee," the sheriff corrected.

"The sheriff's office," she said.

"That's right." He killed the engine and lights and pulled his key from the ignition.

Stacey wanted to ask if she was under arrest, but he hadn't said she was, hadn't read her her rights, so she swallowed the question. No sense putting ideas into his head.

"I've got a couch you can stretch out on, too," he told her. "No offense, but you look like you could use it." His slight smile both apologized and challenged.

"You sweet-talking devil," she told him, batting her eyes before looking away. "Just what a girl wants to hear after a night like this one."

"Don't blame me for tonight," the sheriff said. "You're the one who decided to take a hike."

Stacey nearly snorted but settled for a sniff. She'd taken a hike, all right, and she would dearly love to take another one at that very moment. Unfortunately, she didn't think she'd get very far on crutches. Especially with the way that pain pill the doctor had given her was kicking in. She could feel herself sliding downhill fast.

"On second thought," she told the sheriff, "I think I'll pass on the coffee. What I really need to do is go home."

"Where's home?"

Since he'd killed the engine, the cold was starting to seep into the vehicle. Stacey hugged her coat tighter around herself and lied. "Laramie."

"That's a little out of my territory," the sheriff told her. "We don't have a bus line or passenger train in town. No airline service, either. Since you can't drive, I guess for right now you're going to have to settle for the couch in my office."

Stacey felt herself getting sleepy, courtesy of a night of fresh air and exercise, and the pain pill. At least the sheriff wasn't talking about arresting her. Still, the sooner she parted company with the long arm of the law, the better she would feel, no matter how fascinated she was by his mouth.

"I don't suppose," she said to him, "that since I already owe you for the hospital—did I thank you for that? In case I didn't, thank you."

"You're welcome."

"I can reimburse you as soon as I get my car back and I get my purse out of the trunk."

"We'll get your car in a few hours, when I can get someone to drive it in."

"Thank you." She stared straight ahead, toward the rear door of the courthouse and into its lighted hallway. Anyplace to avoid looking at those lips again. "So, since I'll be paying you back tomorrow, I don't suppose you'd like to lend me a little more. Just enough for a motel room for the night."

He made a low humming sound in his throat, as if he were considering her request. Then, from the corner of her eye, she saw him shake his head.

"I don't suppose so," he said. "I don't think I'll be letting you out of my sight until I talk with the folks at the Flying Ace and see if they want to press charges."

"Charges?" she cried. "Come on, I didn't hurt anything. All I did was walk around in a bunch of sagebrush and pinyon."

"On private property."

"So you say," she grumbled.

"So I know. Come on. There's no sense sitting out here all night. Let's go inside and you can catch a nap while we wait for morning and a decent hour for me to call the ranch."

Stacey gave up. She might as well go inside with him, since she didn't have any other choice.

But she didn't have to like it.

"All right," she finally said. "But I warn you, I'm going to fall asleep."

The courthouse building was old, late eighteenth or early nineteenth century, Stacey guessed, with oak floors that creaked and ceilings that soared, but she didn't get to see much of it, because the door to the sheriff's office, with its black stenciled lettering across frosted glass, was first on the right. Which was fine with her. She was too exhausted and sleepy to tackle, on her unfamiliar crutches, the long hall that bisected the building.

The good news was, she thought as Sheriff Hunk—oh, good grief! She nearly giggled at her Freudian slip. He was a handsome devil, even if he was currently making her life miserable. She'd gotten her first good look at him in the brightly lit hospital. For a moment, there on the exam table, she'd very nearly forgotten the pain in her ankle. She'd been temporarily mesmerized by dark blue eyes that seemed to look right through her.

When he took off his hat, her fingers had actually tingled with the urge to touch his thick black hair. She wanted to know if it was soft or wiry. It looked soft.

His face was broad and strong, with even features and a million-watt smile, when he chose to use it. He'd smiled at the nurses and the doctor, but not at her.

In the car, after leaving the hospital, she hadn't been able to see much but his profile. That's when the strong cut of his lips had grabbed her attention.

Lord, her mind was wandering. She'd had an actual, rational thought in her head a minute ago, before she'd thought of him as Sheriff Hunk.

She nearly giggled at the term.

He was Sheriff *Powell,* Dane Powell, and she'd best be remembering that.

As he held the office door open for her, she realized that her ankle no longer hurt. In fact, she couldn't feel it at all. Not the ankle, not her toes. She wasn't sure, but she thought her eyelids were going numb, too. They kept drooping despite her best efforts to hold them open.

Boy, that was some pain pill.

Through her waning senses, she took in the low wooden railing that separated the entryway from the rest of the office. The sheriff stepped past her and held open a swinging gate for her to pass through.

Inside the office itself Stacey concentrated on working her crutches so they wouldn't slide out from under her on the freshly waxed floor. Around the room sat old wooden desks, only one of which was occupied. There were gray metal file cabinets and beige computer terminals. On the wall she caught a glimpse of wanted posters alongside framed photographs. There was a door marked Wyatt County Sheriff in the far front corner, an unmarked door midway down that wall, and the word *jail* stenciled on the door at the rear of the office.

*Jail.*

He wouldn't dare. Surely he didn't plan to put her in a cell. He still hadn't read her rights to her, hadn't said she was under arrest.

She stopped with the sheriff at the first desk, where he introduced her to the young, freckle-faced man there.

"Donnie, this is Carla Smith."

"How'do, ma'am," Donnie said with a grin and a nod.

"Ms. Smith," Powell said to her, "Deputy Fowler."

"Deputy," she acknowledged.

"Aw, heck, ma'am." His grin was wide, and his face was flushed. "Just call me Donnie."

"Why, thank you." She chanced a glance at the sheriff in time to see him roll his eyes and shake his head.

"Ms. Smith's had a long night, Donnie. She's going to stretch out on the couch in my office for a while."

"Oh, well, sure," Donnie said with a nod and a shuffle. "You go right ahead and have yourself a good rest, and if you need anything, you just call on Donnie, you hear?"

"Why thank you, Dep—I mean Donnie."

"This way," the sheriff said with another roll of his eyes. He pushed open the door to his private office and ushered her inside.

Like the desks out in the open room, his was old and wooden, but larger than the others, and in better condition with fewer nicks and scars. His leather chair was huge, his computer efficient-looking. Two wing chairs in burgundy leather faced his desk, and behind them, against the wall, sat a long matching sofa. The furniture looked expensive.

Stacey frowned. "I thought county sheriffs were notoriously underfunded."

"You thought right." Powell pushed the door closed behind her. "Any particular reason you mention it?"

"I just wondered how the taxpayers feel about your spending their hard-earned dollars on fancy furniture."

"Next thing you're going to tell me is that you work for the governor and were sent here undercover to ferret out waste in the county budget."

She snorted and started toward the couch. She didn't really care what the taxpayers thought at that moment. She was only grateful the couch was there. It looked like heaven to Stacey.

"FYI," the sheriff told her, "the couch and matching chairs, the lamps, and a few other items out in the main room, were donated by generous citizens. The county's tax dollars are safe from abuse. At least by this office. Does that make you feel better?"

Stacey eased down onto the soft leather cushion and let out a long sigh. "Oh, yes. I feel much better now." Still wearing her coat, she put her crutches on the floor and lay down. She curled her arm up beneath her head, closed her eyes and let the pain pill pull her under.

Watching her, Dane was surprised she'd held out as long as she had. The medication had worked fast. He had the strangest urge to smooth that pale lock of hair from her cheek. To carry her home with him and tuck her in bed, where she would be more comfortable and he could take care of her.

The very idea was not only startling, it was appalling, and completely unlike him. Not to mention inappropriate. He was the sheriff, she the...suspect?

No, she wasn't *suspected* of anything. He'd caught her in the act.

Perp?

That made it sound as though she'd held up a liquor store in a police drama on television.

Trespasser. She was that, for certain.

But was she more? If it weren't for the cattle rustling in the area, and if she hadn't hurt herself, he never would have brought her in. He would have put the fear of God into her for taking a hike on someone else's property, then he would have sent her on her way. After calling in her tag number and checking for priors or outstanding warrants, of course. He doubted he'd find either on her.

But there was the matter of the cattle rustlers, and the fact that she'd been lying through her pretty white teeth from the moment he'd asked what she'd been doing out there on the Flying Ace. She'd lied about her name. He'd bet a month's salary that it wasn't Carla Smith, and she probably didn't live in Laramie.

The woman didn't lie worth a damn.

Maybe if she didn't look so much like an innocent angel he wouldn't be trying so hard to figure her out. An uncomfortable angel, he thought, noting the awkward bend of her neck as she slept on his couch. She hadn't even bothered to take off her coat. She'd just more or less keeled over.

A knock sounded quietly on his door.

Dane took off his coat and hung it on the hook next to the door before answering.

It was Donnie, but then, who else could it have been? Dane put a finger to his lips and gave a nod toward the couch.

Donnie leaned forward to peer around the edge of the door. "You said...wow, she's already asleep?" he whispered.

"Yeah. What have you got?"

"Oh. I thought she might want these." The deputy held out a folded gray blanket and a pillow with no pillowcase.

Dane took them, knowing Donnie had gotten them from one of the two cells they kept on this floor for female prisoners. Male prisoners were housed down in the basement.

"Thanks, Donnie," he said, keeping his voice low.

Donnie didn't appear to have heard. He was leaning forward again, staring at their guest with a grin on his face that Dane could only think of as goofy.

"Donnie?"

Donnie finally blinked and straightened. "Huh?"

"I said thanks."

"Oh, yeah. Sure. You're welcome, Sheriff. Who is she? Where'd she come from?"

Dane halfway expected the next question to be, *Can we keep her?* Such was the look on the kid's face. Like he'd just seen the perfect puppy, or horse, or whatever it was that he'd been dreaming of all his life.

"Forget it, Deputy," Dane told him as he nudged him back through the door. "She's way out of your league."

Donnie sighed and grinned. "Don't I know it. But a guy's gotta dream, Sheriff, right? Or else, what's the point?"

"Do your dreaming out at your desk." Dane closed the door on his grinning deputy and shook his head. Donnie was a good kid.

Scratch that. Just because Dane was thirty-five and Donnie was only twenty-three, that didn't make the deputy a kid. He was a man. A young one, but not stupid with it. He'd been on the payroll nearly a year and was doing a good job.

Ordinarily Dane wouldn't have left Donnie alone in the office, not even during the quiet hours of the night. But some damn virus was going around. It had hit three deputies and two jailers, one of whom doubled as a dispatcher, all this week. Another dispatcher was out having gall bladder surgery, and the office manager had quit last week.

With all that going on, Dane felt lucky that Donnie was willing to take the third watch and do double duty as dispatcher and jailer.

But Donnie wasn't the only fairly new staff member in the department. A good portion of Dane's small staff was fairly new on the job, including himself. He'd been sheriff a little more than a year, undersheriff for his predecessor, Gene Martin, for a year before that. It hadn't been three weeks after he'd been sworn in that he'd had to fire two longtime deputies.

He'd known that if he got elected—hell, he'd been a shoe-in, nobody ran against him—he would fire those two. They were cronies of Sheriff Martin's and willing to do anything the man had ordered, no questions asked. The problem with that, Dane thought with disgust, was that not everything Martin ordered was what one would call legal.

Martin had been a popular sheriff for many years, but according to the stories Dane had heard, and what he'd seen for himself the year he worked for the man, Martin had turned into an egotistical bully during his last few years in office. There had been more than a few sighs of relief when he decided not to run for reelection. It had been too bad that when he retired and moved away he hadn't taken his two goons with him.

Deputies Wilson and James had enjoyed throwing their considerable weight around. They weren't above dragging some poor soul off into the dark and beating the hell out of him. They, along with Martin, had done just that to Grady Lewis when he'd come back to town about six months after Dane had taken the job as undersheriff.

When Dane was elected sheriff, he'd decided to wait until Wilson and James pulled something while working for him. It had been a short wait. He'd caught them red-handed rolling a drunk one night behind a bar. He'd fired them on the spot.

It had been a scramble to hire new deputies. He'd lost another due to family business taking him off to another state.

But he had a full complement of ten deputies now, even if some of them were currently out sick. He had a good detective, four honest, tough jailers, two of whom doubled as dispatchers. There were three more on staff whose sole job was dispatching. His two clerks were conscientious, and he hoped whoever he hired as office manager would be the same.

Add them all up and his full staff totaled twenty-one, counting himself. And nobody better forget about the department's two drug-sniffing dogs and their bloodhound, whose specialty was search and rescue.

The only thing missing was an office manager. Marva Dawson quit just last week to help take care of her new grandbaby up in Pine Bluff. He doubted he would ever find anyone who could truly replace her. She'd been the glue that held the department together. She'd known everything about every case they worked, never forgot anything, and had insisted on making the coffee herself.

Where the hell was he going to find someone else like that?

He had a few applications on his desk and a couple of hours to kill before he could call the Flying Ace. He wouldn't feel right calling before seven, even knowing they would all be up and around by five.

Maybe if he could pile on enough paperwork, he could keep his mind off the woman sleeping like a baby on his couch.

The first thing Dane did when he settled at his desk was log onto the Internet and check the social security number Carla Smith had written on the form at the hospital.

It was bogus. No big surprise there, but maybe a little disappointment. For some reason, he kept wanting something, even one small something, about her to be real.

Shaking his head at himself, he put her out of his mind and concentrated on the never-ending pile of paperwork stacked on his desk.

He managed to get some of it taken care of, but not as much as he'd anticipated. He didn't get to work on it until seven, when he planned to call the Flying Ace, because at six, Ace Wilder, manager and part owner of the Flying Ace, called him.

Hearing Ace's voice on the phone, Dane leaned back in his chair and smiled. He had a deep fondness and respect for all four Wilders and their families. Ace was not only one of the most successful ranchers in the state, he was a good friend, as were his brothers, Jack and Trey, and their sister Rachel, and her husband, Grady Lewis.

When Dane had first moved to Hope Springs, the Wilders had gone out of their way to make him feel welcome. Not for any particular reason, but simply because that's the type of people they were. They were his first friends, and were still his best friends. He valued that.

"You read my mind," he said to Ace. "I was just waiting for a decent hour before I called you."

"I hope you didn't have anything important on your mind," Ace said, his voice sounding grim, "because we've got trouble."

Dane straightened in his chair as his stomach dropped to a level somewhere below the basement. He knew what Ace was going to say without hearing it. Still he forced himself to ask, "What's happened?"

"I'm not sure of the exact number, but we're minus somewhere between forty and sixty head of cattle from the south range."

"Son of a bitch."

"That's close to what I said, and a hell of a lot more polite."

"I'm en route. Where do you want me to meet you?" But Dane had a feeling he knew exactly where. Right about the same spot where a fancy little sports car sat parked among the bushes.

"The south road," Ace told him. "You'll see a small sports car parked beneath a tree. Meet us a half mile west of there."

"I'll be there as soon as I can." Dane hung up the phone, but he had to take a deep breath and order himself to relax before his fingers would unclench from the receiver. It was a much longer moment before he could tear his gaze from the woman sleeping so innocently across the room.

Doing his best to ignore her, he picked up the phone again and called John Taylor, the department's detective. After filling him in on the situation and telling him where they were to meet the Wilders, Dane hung up the phone, and once again, his gaze went involuntarily to the woman across the room.

"Carla Smith from Laramie, my Aunt Fanny," he muttered. The angel he'd spotted in the beam of his flashlight mere hours earlier had just moved up a notch—from misdemeanor trespasser caught red-handed, to suspect in a felony cattle-stealing operation.

He wanted to bring her car in. If she had her purse, he could demand to see some ID. If she refused to open her trunk, where she'd stashed her purse and probably her tag, he didn't think he'd have any trouble getting a judge to sign a search warrant, considering the entire population of two counties was up in arms over the cattle rustling.

"Ms. Smith?" He leaned over her and touched her shoulder. "Ms. Smith, can you hear me?"

She scrunched up her face like a pouting angel—did angels pout?—grumbled something unintelligible and made a shooing motion with one limp hand, as if halfheartedly trying to rid herself of a pesky mosquito. Definitely not an angelic gesture.

"It's Sheriff Powell, Ms. Smith."

She frowned and moaned. "Stacey."

Dane stilled. He held his breath. "Stacey?"

"Hmm?" Her eyes were still closed.

"I'm going to go get your car for you."

Without opening her eyes, she smiled, and her face eased. "Care. Sweet."

"Yes. I mean no. I'm going to get your car. But I need your keys."

She worked her mouth, then swallowed. Her smile widened. "Kiss?"

Dane fought a groan. Hell yes, he'd like to kiss her, but he wasn't about to start something with a woman who wasn't even half conscious. "No, keys." He gave her shoulder a small shake. "Where are your keys?"

"Too sleepy to drive." She had yet to open her eyes. Sleep, and probably the painkiller, slurred her words.

Dane didn't know whether to laugh or beat his head against the wall. "I'll drive," he told her. "Just give me your keys so I can bring your car to town."

Her lips pouted; her brow furrowed. "Kiss."

"That'd be real nice, honey, but first give me your keys."

For a long moment he feared she'd drifted back into a deeper sleep. He started to give her shoulder another shake when she spoke again. "Pocket."

"Your keys are in your pocket?"

"S'whadIsaid." She was definitely getting cranky now.

He hoped like hell she meant her coat pocket, or she'd likely sue him for sexual harassment if he had to reach into her jeans. The ice he was skating on, in getting her to provide her keys so he could drive her car, was thin enough. She wasn't exactly aware of what was going on. But there was one more thing he needed from her.

"Do you want me to get your purse out of the trunk?"

"Wannasleep."

"I know, honey, and you can, but do you want your purse?"

She looked as though she was trying to open her eyes, then gave up the struggle. "Yeah. Okay. Purse."

Bingo. Got it. Permission from the suspect to open her trunk.

"Go back to sleep now, honey." Praying for a little more luck, Dane carefully reached into the only coat pocket he could get to without tunneling his hand beneath her, which he'd rather not have to do.

When he reached into her pocket, he came out with more than just her keys. Tangled around his fingers was a wad of ribbon. Upon examination, what he had in his hand was more than two dozen strips of red ribbon, each one about six inches long.

"What the hell?" Adhered to one side of each piece was a strip of reflective tape, and on some of them he found bits of dried sage or pinyon needles.

Now what…?

*Bread crumbs.* He was sure of it. She had tied these pieces of ribbon to bushes and trees and used them to find her way back to her car. They would have picked up the barest glow from her flashlight and would have lit up like neon. Hell, as bright as the moon was last night, they might well have glowed without the flashlight.

"Luckier than Hansel and Gretel, weren't you, angel. Nobody came along behind you and ate your ribbons."

Now he had proof, if he'd needed it, that she

hadn't merely stopped her car and gotten out for a stroll. She had planned and prepared to cross unfamiliar country in the dark.

What Dane wanted to know, and what he thoroughly intended to find out when he got back, was why.

For now, he had her car keys. Getting them, he told himself, was a job well, if not exactly fairly, done.

Now, what the hell was he supposed to do with her while he was gone? He was likely to be out for three hours or more. If he left her sleeping like she was on the couch she might never be able to move her neck again, the way it was scrunched up at an odd angle.

He eased one arm beneath her neck and stuffed the pillow Donnie had brought beneath her head. "There," he said aloud to himself. "That's better."

"Hmm," she murmured. Then, before Dane realized what was happening, she raised her arms and wrapped them around his neck. Her eyes fluttered open, then closed. "Kiss now."

He wanted to. Oh, yes, indeed, he wanted to taste that sweet-looking mouth. But she was too out of it to know what she was saying, and she was in his custody. In his care. He could not, would not allow himself to take advantage of her.

Then she pulled him down and parted her lips against his.

He could have pulled away. Probably. Maybe. Until he heard the soft moan that slid up her throat. It echoed the same pleasure he felt. Her mouth was soft and sweet, hot and hungry. He did his best to give her what she asked for, and in the process, took what she offered.

No, dammit, he couldn't do this. When he kissed this woman he wanted her wide-awake and aware of him. As aware of him as he was of her.

Just one more taste. One more slide of his tongue along hers.

Then her arms fell from around his neck and her mouth went slack.

Dane pulled back. "Stacey?"

She smiled and snuggled deeper into the pillow, as deeply asleep as he'd ever seen anyone. He didn't know whether to be insulted, amused or relieved.

He was all of those things. Insulted, of course, because no woman had ever fallen into such a state of unconsciousness while he was kissing her. Amused because it served him right that she'd fallen asleep. Relieved because he shouldn't have been kissing her in the first place, and he had high hopes that when she woke she wouldn't remember it.

Biting back a curse, he stood and looked down at that angelic face. For all he knew, he'd just been kissing a cattle-rustling felon. He shook his head at himself and walked away. When he left his office a moment later he closed the door softly behind him.

"Is she still asleep?" Donnie asked.

"That's affirmative. When she wakes up, I'm counting on you not to let her leave."

Donnie swallowed and bobbed his head. "Yes, sir. Does that mean you're heading out again?"

"I am. No matter what she says, she stays here until I get back. Copy that?"

"I copy, Sheriff. Is she under arrest?"

"Not yet. I've got to get to the Flying Ace. It

seems they're missing some cattle this morning,'' Dane added grimly.

''Ah, damn.'' Donnie, along with all the other deputies, was well aware of the situation with the rustlers. They'd all been hoping they'd get lucky and the culprits would bypass their county.

It appeared their luck had just run out.

''Yeah,'' Dane said. ''Damn.''

## Chapter Three

Along the south border of the Flying Ace ranch, a mere half mile from the little red sports car, the fence had been cut.

Jack Wilder, ranch foreman and the second oldest of the Wilder siblings, had awakened early that morning. Unable to go back to sleep for worrying about the possibility of rustlers, he'd taken a ranch rig and started driving the outer fences.

He took the ranch road up into the foothills, then turned south along the west edge of Wilder property. He saw nothing amiss, and at the southwest corner he turned east, coming down out of the foothills on what the locals called South Flying Ace Road. The land was more rugged on the south side of the ranch, so he drove slowly as he kept one eye on the gravel road and one on the barbed wire fence that kept Flying Ace beef on Flying Ace land. And hopefully kept everyone else out.

It was the sight of a fast-food sack that made him stop. The sky had still been dark, but a flutter of white, snagged on the barbed wire, caught Jack's attention. He'd stopped and found that the fence had been cut and heavy tire tracks, like those made by a semi, led through the opening.

Then there was the sack itself, with its distinctive logo recognized around the world. The nearest location for that particular franchise was at least a hundred miles south.

Jack had used his cell phone and called his brother at the main house. By then the sky was lightening in the east. He didn't wait for his brother, but set out on foot, careful not to disturb the tracks.

By the time Dane arrived, Jack pretty much had the situation figured out. Grimly he filled the sheriff and detective in on what he'd found.

Dane, who was used to doing his own detective work back on the L.A. police force, kept an eagle eye on John Taylor as the county detective took photos, drew sketches and made notes.

John was fifty-three, happily divorced and bald as a cue ball. The latter, he claimed, was a direct result of the former. His ex, he said, took everything, including the hair on his head. He was a good detective and came to Wyatt County with four years as a detective on the Denver P.D. under his belt.

Dane wasn't hovering because he doubted the man's ability, but more because as sheriff, he took this cattle rustling personally. But he was careful not to interfere. He let John do his job and helped or gave advice only when asked. John knew Dane's restraint came hard, since the sheriff had once been a detective himself, so he cut Dane some slack and asked his opinion often, swearing that two heads were better than one.

The two of them examined the cut in the fence. John took the paper sack as evidence, and they walked with Ace, Jack and their younger brother Trey the two miles into the ranch, to the spot where the rustlers had parked their truck and loaded the cattle.

"Fifty head, you think?" Dane asked.

Tight-lipped with fury, Ace Wilder nodded. "Near as we can tell."

The thieves had come prepared. In addition to the semi, there had also been a pickup pulling a horse trailer. They'd rounded up the cattle on horseback and herded them into the funnel they'd erected with portable fencing. The marks on the ground told the story.

"Damn, I'm sorry," Dane said with feeling.

"So are we," Ace said. "But I hope you aren't apologizing for not preventing this."

That was exactly what Dane was doing, but he refrained from admitting it and simply shrugged.

"Hell, Dane, it's a big county," Jack said. "You can't be everywhere at once."

"No," Dane admitted. "But I was here. Last night, around two."

"Here?" Trey asked.

Dane nodded toward the east. "Picked up a woman trespassing on your ranch." Picked her up, carried her, kissed her.

"The sports car?" Ace asked.

"Yeah." He sighed heavily. "I think I've got some new questions for that lady."

"You think she's involved in this?"

"I don't believe in coincidence," Dane said. "Not the kind where two separate crimes occur at the same time, in the same place."

"What was her story when you picked her up?"

Dane smirked. "Said she was looking for night-blooming cactus."

The response from the Wilders and John Taylor was a round of laughing snorts and remarks of disbelief.

"Yeah," Dane said. "That's pretty much what I thought, too." He led the men to the place where he'd first spotted her. "John, why don't you see if you can backtrack along her trail. I'd be real curious to know where she went, and if she met with the rustlers."

"Will do, Sheriff. Jack, you're a better tracker. Wanna give me a hand? Or an eye?"

"As a matter of fact," Jack said, settling his hat more firmly on his head, "I do."

"Here." Dane reached into his coat pocket and pulled out a piece of ribbon. "She's got a pocketful of these. I figure she used them like the proverbial bread crumbs. She obviously picked up after herself on her way back, but she might have missed one or two."

John eyed the ribbon and its reflective tape. "Pretty clever of somebody just out looking for cactus."

"Yeah," Dane said heavily. "That's what I thought."

By now Dane had already been gone from the office nearly three hours. He knew it would be another hour or two before John and Jack had answers for him, and he was getting antsy about the woman in his office. It wasn't that he didn't trust Donnie to keep her there, but Donnie had gone off duty more than an hour ago, and sometimes instructions got skewed when passed along. And besides that, stuff just happened.

No, it wasn't Donnie or anyone on his staff he didn't trust. It was the woman. No matter how much he enjoyed kissing her.

"I'm going to head back to the office," he told his detective. "Call me on my cell phone instead of the radio the minute you know anything." He didn't want to chance having Ms. Smith—Carla? Stacey? Whoever she was—overhear whatever John might have to say if he called in on the radio.

John nodded. "Will do."

When Stacey woke, she had trouble opening her eyes. God, she felt like she'd been drugged.

Slowly the memories returned, and with them, she groaned.

The long, long walk over rough, unfamiliar ground, most of it in the dark. The duty her grandmother had sent her to see to. The longer walk back. The blinding light. The fall. *The sheriff.*

Dane Powell. Oh, yes, she remembered him, all right. He was the reason she was injured, the reason she was on crutches. The reason she wasn't home at this very minute in her own bed instead of scrunched up on a leather sofa, no matter how pretty it was.

She tried opening her eyes again, but they didn't seem to want to cooperate. That was the pain pill she remembered taking. She always woke up groggy after taking medication, which was why she rarely took any. But she remembered the vicious pain; the pill had been justified.

She might have given up and slipped back into sleep but for the sudden memory of a kiss that had warmed her from the inside out. *That* had her eyes popping open wide. She jackknifed to a sitting position, then grabbed her head and moaned at the stabbing pain caused by the abrupt movement.

One little-bitty pain pill, and she had the worst hangover of her life. In fact, it was the first and only hangover of her life, and it just didn't seem fair that she hadn't gotten to party first.

Or had she? The memory of kissing Dane Powell seemed startlingly real. She swore she could still taste him on her lips. But it couldn't be real. It must have been a dream. Maybe, if she wanted to be honest, it was merely wishful thinking.

She didn't think she wanted to be that honest.

But unless she'd misread the man entirely, and she didn't think she had, he would not have taken advantage of her in such a manner. She'd been asleep. Essentially helpless, and in his custody. Not only did he seem to her to have too much integrity for such a stunt, but also he was too smart to leave himself open to a charge of sexual harassment.

Therefore, she must have dreamed the kiss. It simply could not have happened. The very idea made her break out in a sweat. That, plus she still wore her coat, and the office was plenty warm.

After struggling out of her coat, she retrieved her crutches from the floor, groaned her way upright and made her way to the door. The first face she saw when she opened the door was Deputy Donnie. She was proud of herself for remembering his name when so much of what happened after meeting him was nothing more than a haze.

"You're awake." The deputy beamed at her as though her being awake was something particularly clever. "Good morning."

She returned the greeting in a scratchy voice.

It was midmorning and the office gave evidence that other people had come on duty since she'd fallen asleep on the sheriff's couch. A half-empty coffee mug sat on one desk, a half-eaten bagel on another. A uniformed officer sat talking on the phone at the dispatcher's desk at the front of the office.

"That's Sergeant Bates," Donnie told her. "He does double duty as a jailer and dispatcher. I'll introduce you when he gets off the phone."

Stacey made a humming sound of agreement, but her mind wasn't on introductions. "The sheriff is gone?" she asked.

Donnie nodded. "Yes, ma'am."

"Was he going to get my car?" She had some vague memory of a discussion about her car keys, but it was too fuzzy in her head to make sense. She reached to check for her keys, but realized she'd left her coat on the sofa in the sherriff's office.

"I don't know, ma'am," Donnie said. "I know he had to go out to the Flying Ace."

She nodded. "That's where my car was."

"Then I expect he'll get one of the Wilders to drive it back to town for you."

Stacey started to say she'd be grateful to whoever drove her car to town, even if it was a Wilder, but about the time she opened her mouth, her stomach let out an audaciously loud rumble. She place a hand over her abdomen and smiled ruefully.

Donnie blushed and did a shuffle thing with his feet. "I guess you're probably hungry." He frowned and looked over at the small table that held the coffeemaker. "The bagels and donuts are all gone." Then his face brightened. "I could go get you something from the café."

"Oh, could you?" She reached out and placed a hand on his arm. "That would be wonderful. But... until the sheriff gets back with my purse—"

"The sheriff has your purse?"

"It was in the trunk of my car. It's a long story," she said. "Anyway, I don't have any money on me, so I guess I'll make do with coffee for now, if you have some to spare."

"Sure," he said eagerly. "Sure. We've got plenty of coffee. But I can't let you go hungry. You can pay me back when the sheriff gets here. Or better yet, I'll take it out of petty cash. I know the sheriff won't mind."

Stacey figured she knew otherwise, but she didn't say so. She was hungry, and she was tired of letting the sheriff call all the shots, especially when he wasn't around. "Are you sure you wouldn't mind?" she asked Donnie.

"Of course not," he said. "Just tell me what you want and I'll call it in over at the café. That'll save a little time, since you're so hungry and all."

"Donnie, you're a prince."

Grinning, he blushed to the roots of his hair.

Dane pulled out onto the highway headed back to town and glanced in his rearview mirror. Behind him roared the snazzy little sports car, with Ace Wilder at the wheel, grinning like an idiot.

Dane thought of it as a little car, because it was so much smaller than his Blazer. But once Ace moved the driver's seat back there'd been plenty of room for his long legs. The man was having the time of his life driving that car. Dane was more than a little envious.

He'd left John and Jack to follow Stacey/Carla Smith's trail and see where it led. He would have gone with them, but he didn't want to leave her to Donnie any longer than necessary.

He reached for his radio mic. "Unit one to dispatch."

When more than a few seconds went by and no one answered, Dane frowned. Donnie might have gone home, since he was off duty now, or he might have stayed around to wait for Dane. In either case, Stan would be in by now, and the day shift of deputies would have come in. They wouldn't have gone off and left the office unattended.

"Unit one to dispatch," he said again.

"Go ahead, unit one."

Dane took his eyes off the road and stared at the radio speaker. There must be something wrong with it, because for a minute there, it had sounded as if Ms. Stacey/Carla Smith herself had been speaking.

Damn, she must be weighing more heavily on his mind than he'd realized, if Stan's voice could sound like hers to his ears.

"I'm ten-eight and on my way in," he said.

"Copy that, Mr. Sheriff."

Dammit all to hell and back, that *was* her. "Ms. Smith, this is an official police radio, not a toy."

"Ten-four," came her reply. "I should have said, copy that, unit one. Is that better?"

"Where," Dane said carefully, "is Stan?"

"Who—oh, you meant Sergeant Bates?"

"Yes." Dane found it difficult to speak while grinding his teeth, and he couldn't really bang his head on anything while driving sixty miles an hour down the highway. "I mean Sergeant Bates. My dispatcher."

"He's also your jailer, and he's tending to a prisoner downstairs in the jail."

Dane glared at the speaker. "Stan left you—a civilian—alone to man the radio?" He still couldn't believe it.

"I volunteered. Donnie would have done it, but he's down at the café picking up my breakfast."

"He's what?" Dane could practically see her. If they were having this conversation face-to-face she would be batting those baby blues at him. He could feel the vein in his temple start to throb. "He's what?" Dane repeated a little more calmly.

"He's gone to get my breakfast. According to the duty roster here, he's off the clock, so you can't get mad at him for leaving his post. He wasn't here, and one of your deputies brought in a prisoner who was so rowdy it took both the deputy and Sergeant Bates to get him down the stairs. So I volunteered to man the radio."

Dane unclenched his jaw just enough to speak. "Then volunteer to write this down. Unit One is ten-seventeen—that's *en route*—to the office."

"Copy that." She said it easily, as if she'd been manning the radio for years. "Unit One is ten-seventeen to the office."

"That means I'm on my way."

"I know what it means, Sheriff. You have this convenient list of ten codes right here next to the radio."

"Good. Then look up ten-three and do it."

"That would be...ten-three, stop transmitting. Ten-four to that. Dispatch out."

"And don't touch anything else," he added. "Unit One out."

Son of a... Dane was going to wring someone's neck for this. Hearing two different sets of clicks on the radio, indicating that two people, probably his deputies, were laughing at the exchange that just took place, did not help Dane's mood. But considering who he'd had the exchange with, one of those sets of clicks could have been from her. Damn her lying little self.

And to think that he'd been attracted to her.

He flipped on his lights and siren and stepped on the gas. That fancy little sports car of hers shouldn't have any trouble keeping up.

Stacey's grin was huge as she sat back in the chair at the dispatcher's desk. Oh, County Sheriff Dane Powell hadn't liked that, no, sir, he hadn't. And anything he didn't like just tickled her pink. It was time she took control of things from his hands. She didn't like men who were controlling, never had, never would. Give her a sweetheart like Deputy Call-me-Donnie Fowler anyday. Now *there* was a nice man. If a woman had to have a man around, and if that man simply *had* to be a cop.

She had no doubt that when the sheriff walked through the door he was going to have steam coming out his ears. She hoped Sergeant Bates didn't get into too much trouble for leaving her in charge of the radio. But really, what else could he have done? The prisoner the other deputy had brought in had been drunk and belligerent and working his way up to out-and-out violent. No telling what would have happened if he'd had to handle the man on his own so the deputy could man the radio.

A few minutes later Donnie returned with her breakfast. When she explained about Sergeant Bates, Donnie thanked her for filling in and took over from her.

"You might not want to be sitting there when the sheriff gets back," she warned. "He wasn't exactly thrilled when he called in and I answered."

Donnie pursed his lips, but soon gave up and grinned. "He can't yell at me. I'm not even on duty. But I'll warn the sergeant."

"Thanks. I thought you should know. And thanks for getting me the breakfast."

His cheeks turned beet-red. "Aw, heck, Ms. Smith, you're welcome."

She nearly told him to call her Stacey. Heavens, that wouldn't do. Not when he thought her name was Carla.

This business of lying was getting complicated.

She took her breakfast to the sheriff's office, made herself at home again on his burgundy leather sofa and dug in. Using crutches evidently stimulated her appetite; she felt as if she could eat an entire steer.

From where she sat she couldn't see into the outer office, but she heard Sergeant Bates and the other deputy come back upstairs. She caught bits and pieces of their conversation with Donnie and knew

Donnie had warned the sergeant that the sheriff was not pleased. The sergeant didn't seem too worried, from what little Stacey could hear.

She wondered about that. Was Bates not worried because he didn't care what the sheriff thought, because he had no respect for the man, if not the office he held? Or was his lack of concern based on friendship with and trust in the man he worked for, trust that Dane would be fair and listen to him before doing anything drastic?

She would be interested to see how this turned out.

Not long after she finished eating, the sheriff returned. He didn't exactly storm through the door—at least the frosted glass didn't break—but he came in with an attitude. Stacey had been leaning on her crutches in his office doorway just so she wouldn't miss his entrance.

And he made an entrance, all right. What an entrance. For a moment Stacey thought she was seeing double. The man who came in with him had that same coal-black hair, those same vivid blue eyes, the same strong, square, don't-mess-with-me jaw. The two men could have been brothers.

Heck, for all Stacey knew, they were. The other man was a few years older, judging by the extra lines fanning out from his eyes. Lines that did nothing to detract from the strong, handsome face.

But it was the sheriff who drew her attention. When he looked across the room and their gazes met, and she felt the skin on the back of her neck prickle with physical awareness—of the male-female variety—she almost wished she had missed his entrance. Almost, but not quite. The sharp, sexual zing that zipped through her startled her, amazed her, even thrilled her. She didn't think she'd ever felt something so powerful from merely looking a man in the eye.

But she also felt frightened, threatened. Not physically. She didn't think the man was going to cross the room and hit her. But the look in his eyes, for the shortest of seconds, said he might like to cross the room and kiss her.

His gaze lowered to her mouth as though he knew that she had dreamed of kissing him.

Oh, yes, she thought as a shiver that had nothing to do with cold and everything to do with heat raced down her spine. Terrifying.

Dane stared at her lips and nearly reeled. What the hell was it with him, that he could want to kiss her and strangle her, maybe even arrest her, all at the same time? He could swear her taste still lingered on his lips.

Sleep deprivation, that's what this craziness was. He hadn't had more than a thirty-minute nap in two days. All he needed was a good night's sleep and he'd be his old self again. He would be able to look at the woman across the room with the cool detachment she deserved.

But he couldn't wait for that good night's sleep. He had to dredge up a little cool reserve right here and now.

He tore his gaze from her, aware that Ace, behind him, and Donnie and Stan before him, were giving him funny looks. He ignored their looks and turned to Stan.

"I hear you had trouble with a prisoner?"

"Jim had to help me get Harley downstairs so he

could sleep it off. You know how mean he gets when he ties one on.''

Dane grunted. Harley Schmidt was a frequent guest in their humble establishment. He was a big man, and a mean drunk. No wonder Stan had needed help and had to leave Carla, or Stacey or whoever she was, out here to catch the radio. If she hadn't volunteered to help, Dane's call would have gone unanswered for quite a while, and he would have been worried as hell.

"I was lucky Ms. Smith offered to man the desk while Jim and I were downstairs. Yours was the only call she got. She did real fine, don't you think?''

Dane's only answer was a grunt. Stan was right, it had been nice of her to help out. But that didn't mean he had to like it.

He looked at Donnie. "What are you still doing still here?''

"Heck, Sheriff, you said I was supposed to…'' He looked over at the woman, then quickly away.

That's what Dane had thought. He'd told Donnie to make sure she stayed put, so Donnie had stayed to make sure she did. Of course, she could have left at any time while Donnie was gone and Stan and Jim were downstairs.

She wouldn't have gotten far without her car, and on crutches. She must have realized that she was good and stuck. Dane couldn't think of any other reason she stayed, given her eagerness to depart his company last night.

"Thanks for staying, Donnie," Dane said. "I appreciate it. Consider it overtime.''

"Hey, thanks, Sheriff.''

"Don't mention it. You can take off now. Ace?''

Dane motioned for Ace to follow him as he started toward his office, and the woman waiting there for him.

Dane stopped before her and made a sweeping motion toward the door with his arm. "After you, Ms. Smith."

She batted her eyes. "Why, thank you, Sheriff." She turned and made her way on her crutches to one of the wing chairs before his desk.

He motioned for Ace to take the other wing chair, then went behind his desk and sat down.

She smiled at Ace, then glanced down at the purse he carried in his hand. "Not that I think your masculinity suffers any from your carrying a purse," she told him, nearly laughing, "but it really doesn't go with those boots." She held her hand out. "I'll take it now. Thanks for bringing it."

Before he handed over the purse, Ace looked to Dane.

Dane nodded, and Ace passed it over.

"This means you brought my car to town?" she asked Dane.

"Thank Ace. He drove it in. This is Ace Wilder, by the way. It was his land you were trespassing on last night."

She eyed Ace with a look that was half surprise, half mistrust. "Sheriff," she said, "I told you, I didn't know I was on private property."

Dane raised one finger. "Hold that thought." He turned to the computer beside him and logged onto the Internet. In less than a minute he had what he was looking for.

"Ace, I'd like you to meet Stacey C. Landers, of Cheyenne."

The woman before him nearly came out of her chair. Outrage radiated from every inch of her. "You opened my purse? You *opened* my *purse* and went *through* it? How dare—"

Dane held up a hand to stop her. "I didn't open your purse. First, in case you've forgotten, you told me before I left to call you Stacey." *Right before you kissed the hell out of me.*

"I did not," she claimed.

Dane arched a brow. It was entirely possible that she didn't remember demanding that he kiss her, then taking matters into her own hands. He didn't much care for that idea, but it was possible.

"You did," he told her. "But even if you hadn't, I checked your license tag. Just now. On the computer. You saw me do it. The tag was in the trunk with your purse. I put it back on the bumper where it belongs, by the way. It's against the law to drive without one."

With her lips drawn up like she'd been sucking on a green persimmon, she glared at him. Then she sighed and threw her hands in the air. "Okay, I'm Stacey Landers. You got me, copper. Now what are you going to do with me?"

"The answer depends on how forthcoming you are."

"Forthcoming with what?"

"Answers to the questions I'm about to ask you."

She grinned, but there was tension behind it. "You gonna grill me, copper?"

"Last night I asked you what you were doing out there on private property. I want a straight answer."

She opened her mouth, but he cut her off.

"Before you go giving me any more nonsense

about looking for night-blooming cactus you should be aware that we know cattle rustlers hit the Flying Ace last night, about a half mile from where you parked your car. You're in big trouble, lady. I suggest you start talking.''

## Chapter Four

Stacey could do no more than gape at the sheriff for a long moment. "Rustlers?" Her voice felt as raspy as it sounded in her ears. "Those men were stealing cattle?"

"Are you going to tell me you weren't helping them?" the sheriff demanded.

"*Helping* them?" Stacey cried. "I spent half the night *hiding* from them. If it hadn't been for them being in my way, I would have been gone long before you came by."

"What do you mean, they were in your way?"

"Just what I said." Oh, she wanted to wipe that look of suspicion and disbelief off his face. She'd never been treated this way—as if she were some sort of criminal—in her life. But then, under the circumstances, she couldn't exactly say she blamed him. The entire situation stank to high heaven, and she was right smack in the middle of it.

She'd like to wring Gran's neck for getting her into this, but at the same time she was thankful that it wasn't Gran sitting here with her foot throbbing while the sheriff put the thumbscrews to her.

"Explain," Powell said. "What men? How were they in your way?"

Stacey swallowed. This was a little more than she'd been prepared to deal with. Cattle rustling was serious business, as in felony. She would keep Gran's secret for as long as she could, but if push came to shove, Stacey would spill whatever was necessary to stay clear of anything to do with cattle rustling.

She swallowed again. "It was just before full dark," she said, replaying the event in her mind. "I was...out walking, like I said, and I crested a ridge, and there they were."

"There who were? What did you see?"

"There was a big tractor-trailer rig. A semi, you know? A cattle hauler. And there was a pickup with a horse trailer behind it. They used two horses. And they had this pipe fencing set up to funnel the cattle into the back of the big trailer."

"How many men?"

"I'm not sure. There were the two on horseback and two others that I saw."

"If you saw them again, would you be able to identify them?"

"Probably not the two on horseback. They had their hats pulled low and one of them wore a bandanna over his face, like an Old West bank robber."

"What about the other two?"

Stacey didn't even have to think. "I'd recognize them."

"You'd be able to identify them?"

"Yes."

"Could you describe them to a police sketch artist?"

"Yes."

The sheriff leaned back in his chair and folded his arms across his chest. He studied her as if she were a bug under a microscope. He was, she assumed, trying to decide whether or not she was telling the truth.

That was exactly what Dane was attempting to determine. If she was in cahoots with the rustlers, she could easily "identify" or "describe" the wrong men and throw Dane off the scent. And if she wasn't in cahoots with them, what the hell had she been doing out there? That was a question she had yet to answer with anything he could believe.

He had asked her before, several times. This time he'd go at it sideways. "What did you mean, you had to hide from them because they were in your way?"

"Just what I said. I needed to cross the area where they were parked. I had to hide behind some rocks, until my legs went numb waiting for them to leave."

"Why?" Dane asked.

She heaved a sigh, as if to say the answer should be obvious even to an imbecile. "So they wouldn't see me."

"No, why did you need to cross that particular area?"

"Because I was the chicken and it was the road."

She bared her teeth and batted her lashes. "I wanted to get to the other side."

"Your sarcasm is misplaced, Ms. Landers," Dane warned her. "Cattle rustling is a felony."

"I'm aware of that."

"Were you their lookout?"

"Of course not," she cried.

"Their scout, maybe? You sneaked around and found the best spot for them?"

"Don't be ridiculous."

From the corner of his eye Dane saw Ace frown and narrow his eyes. "What's on your mind?" Dane asked.

Ace slowly turned his head and looked at the woman. He took a long look, clear down to her feet. Then he looked at Dane with a half smile. Reaching for the cell phone on his belt, he said, "Hold that thought."

Ace placed a call by pressing a single button on the phone. That told Dane he was calling someone he called often. One of the family, probably.

"It's me," Ace said into the phone. "How'd you make out on the trail? Uh-huh. Lost it, huh? Take a run up to the cemetery and see if you don't pick it up. And while you're there...yeah. Call me as soon as you know."

Dane didn't need an explanation. He and Ace both eyed Stacey with new speculation.

The Flying Ace ranch had its own private cemetery where family members and longtime employees were buried. Dane had heard the story more than once from the Wilders about the time when Ace was a boy and Stoney, their foreman, found a dead man out on the range. The man had no identification on him; the sheriff back then apparently tried for months to figure out who the man was, but never did. Meanwhile, King Wilder, Ace's father, had the man buried with a blank headstone in the family cemetery.

Since then, two or three times a year, someone had been sneaking up to the cemetery and leaving flowers and other items on the stranger's grave. The Wilders had never been able to learn who was doing it, only that whoever it was hiked in from the road rather than driving past the ranch headquarters.

Hiked in from the road, just as had one Stacey C. Landers.

Beneath his and Ace's steady gazes, the woman in question stared resolutely at the corner of Dane's desk.

"You're awfully quiet all of a sudden," Dane said to her.

She glanced up, then away. "I've got nothing to say."

"Ace pegged it, didn't he?"

"I don't know what you're talking about."

"What was it this time?" Dane asked. "Flowers?"

She gave a blank, deadpan look. "I don't know what you're talking about."

"I'm curious about something," Dane said.

"I'm sure you are," she muttered.

"Why didn't you tell me last night that you saw men stealing cattle?"

"How was I supposed to know they were stealing them?" she cried. "I watch the news and read books. I know ranchers haul cattle around all the time. I thought it was him." She waved a hand toward Ace.

"You thought it was Ace? One of the men you saw looked like him?"

"No, none of them looked like him." She said it as though any simpleton should know better. "I just thought somebody was moving their own cattle to someplace else."

"In the dark?"

"It wasn't quite dark yet. It never occurred to me they were rustlers. Rustlers." She let out a short, wry chuckle. "In my experience, rustlers are bad guys in old black-and-white Westerns, not real people."

"Don't I wish," Dane said. "But if you thought these men were legitimate, why did you hide from them?"

Again she looked at him as though she had serious doubts about his intelligence. When she spoke, she pronounced each word slowly and distinctly. "So they wouldn't know I was there."

"Why didn't you want anyone to know you were there? You already told me you had no idea you were on private property."

"I also told me you my name was Carla Smith."

"Yeah." Dane sat back again and folded his arms across his chest. "You did. Why?"

"Because I wasn't hurting anything and I didn't figure it was any of your business what my name was, or what I was doing out there."

"What *were* you doing out there?"

For someone who could fire back an answer as fast as anyone Dane had ever seen, she could clam up just as fast.

He resisted the urge to swear, but just barely. "Since you've lied about everything else all night long, maybe you're still lying. Maybe you were working with the rustlers. Have you ever been arrested? Keep in mind that I can check that out easily enough.''

The glare she shot him might have felled a lesser man. Dane prided himself on taking it without a blink.

''No,'' she informed him, ice forming on every word. ''I have never been arrested. Check all you want.''

''What,'' he asked her again, ''were you doing out there last night?''

Again she spoke slowly, clearly, pronouncing each word with care. ''Looking for night-blooming cactus.''

Dane pursed his lips. It was surely perverse of him to like a woman—a suspect—who could sit there and lie to him, but damn if he wasn't liking her more by the minute. ''Did you know that the tops of your ears turn red when you lie?''

With cheeks flaming, she gave her head a shake until her hair covered her ears.

Beside her, Ace chuckled. ''If you two will excuse me, I think now's a good time for me to help myself to some county coffee. Anybody else want some?''

''Yes, please,'' Stacey said.

''Count me in,'' Dane answered.

While Ace Wilder was out of the room, Stacey listened as the sheriff placed a long-distance call and spoke to someone about getting a sketch artist to come work with her on sketches of the cattle rustlers. She heard him offer to drive her to Cheyenne so the artist wouldn't have to travel. Stacey held her breath, hoping against hope that he would do just that. The sooner she got away from Dane Powell the better she would like it. If he took her to Cheyenne she would do her thing with the sketch artist and that would be that. Once Dane left, these disturbingly hot, itchy feelings inside her would go away.

But apparently the idea of taking her to Cheyenne didn't work. When the sheriff hung up the phone, he told her it would be a couple of days before anyone could come.

"A couple of days?" she protested. "You don't mean to keep me here that long."

He shrugged. "You can't drive yet, not with that ankle. You're more or less stuck here anyway. We've got a nice little motel just down the street. I'm sure they've got room for you. Unless, of course, you prefer a cell in the back room."

"You're not locking me up." She practically growled the words.

"Not if I don't have to. But even if you're not a suspect—and that's still iffy—you're a material witness to a felony, and I need you to ID the rustlers. So you'll stay here for the time being."

"Why couldn't we go to Cheyenne and get it over with?" she asked, a touch of desperation creeping into her voice.

"Because their software is being upgraded and everyone who uses it is in training."

"Whatever happened to the old-fashioned artists—the ones who actually draw things without the help of a computer?"

"Oh, the state bureau's got one of those, but he's up in Gillette. They've had some man hanging around an elementary school up there, spooking the kids. He's working with them to come up with a likeness."

"I guess," Stacey said, "in the overall scheme of things, some pervert hanging around a grade school is a little more important than cattle rustlers."

"Something like that."

Conversation ran out, but that didn't keep the sheriff from watching every breath she took, every move she made.

Stacey stared resolutely at the front corner of his desk. She refused to look up and meet that mocking grin she knew she would find on Dane Powell's face. Or more accurately, that mouth she swore she could still taste.

Stacey had never been a good liar, but she thought she'd been pulling it off pretty well until he found out her real name. If only she hadn't fallen and hurt herself last night when he'd blinded her with his flashlight.

If only she hadn't let Gran talk her into coming out to Wyatt County in the first place.

*Yeah, yeah, if only.*

Okay, she was here, albeit half-crippled, and under suspicion. All she had to do was figure a way out of this mess and she could be gone. Somehow.

Obviously she was going to have to cooperate with the sheriff. At least, as much as her word to Gran would allow.

Of course, she'd promised Gran she wouldn't be seen by anyone, and she'd sure blown that. Which raised a question in her mind.

She lifted her head and looked at the sheriff. "Just out of curiosity, what made you come looking for me with your handy-dandy little flashlight last night, anyway?"

One corner of his mouth quirked, and his eyes

danced. "Police business. And I'll have you know that's a county-issue, heavy-duty, industrial strength Maglite."

"Ah."

"Ah?"

Stacey smirked. "A testosterone flashlight."

He chuckled. "Good one, Ms. Landers."

"Oh, please. Aren't we friends? You can call me Stacey."

"Or Carla?"

She gave her eyelid muscles another workout and batted her eyes. "Stacey will be fine. Dane."

"If you're not going to tell me what you were doing on the Flying Ace last night, you can call me Sheriff Powell."

"I guess that answers that," she said fatally.

"Answers what?"

"We're definitely not friends."

"Oh, I don't know." His voice slid low and deep, sending shivers down her spine—shivers of heat that were somehow reflected in the blue of his eyes when he looked at her. "You seemed to like me well enough last night."

Moisture pooled in Stacey's mouth until she had to swallow or drool. She chose to swallow. "I don't…"

"Don't remember?" His smile spoke of intimate secrets and stole her breath. "I'm not surprised. You were pretty much out of it from that pain pill when you grabbed me."

"When *I* grabbed *you?*"

"Don't worry." His smile widened. "I didn't mind at all. In fact, you can feel free to grab me and kiss me again—"

"*Kiss* you?" Had she done that? Had she actually *done* that?

"—anytime you want."

"When pigs fly." She wanted nothing more at that moment than to deny that she had kissed him, but the fog was lifting from her memory. Not completely, for which she thought she might be eternally grateful, but enough to allow her to recall slipping her arms around a strong, warm neck, pulling his face down to hers...and...oh, good grief!

"But," he told her, "just because I enjoyed being kissed by you—"

"Did you, now," she said archly. Might as well go with it, she decided, since there didn't seem to be any use in denying it.

"Very much," he said with another smile. "But that doesn't mean I won't charge you."

"With what?" she cried. Her mind was still on that kiss. Now he was talking about charges, and she had to play catch-up. "The most you can charge me with is trespassing, if Mr. Wilder decides to press charges." And from what she knew of the Wilders— which wasn't much, but what there was wasn't good—he just might.

As if on cue, Ace Wilder stepped into the room balancing three mugs of coffee. "Who am I pressing charges against?" he asked as he doled out the mugs.

"You should think about whether or not you want to press charges against Ms. Landers for trespassing."

Stacey blew on the surface of her coffee and eyed the man who'd just given it to her. He wouldn't press charges. Surely he wouldn't.

"I'll have to think about it."

That was not exactly the answer Stacey had been hoping for, but it would do for the time being.

Just then the sheriff's cell phone chirped. He answered it and spoke in short, terse phrases that didn't mean much to Stacey, except that she gathered he was talking to one of his deputies.

When he ended the call, he eyed Stacey critically, then looked at Ace. "Well," he said. "I now know what she was doing on your ranch last night, and you now know who your mysterious graveyard visitor is. You can add a bottle of Jim Beam to your list of items left on the stranger's grave."

Stacey felt trapped. If it wasn't for her injured ankle, which was hurting more and more by the minute, she might seriously consider bolting for the door. But what good would that do? And really, if she was careful, everything could still work out all right.

She was puzzled, however, by the slow smile that curved Ace Wilder's mouth. He actually looked pleased about the situation, which was not what she would have expected.

"So," Wilder said, "you're our stealth grave decorator. It's good to finally meet you. Does this mean the man in the grave's name is Landers?"

Stacey wasn't sure exactly why Gran had always been so adamant that no one learn that the man in the Wilders' grave was Grandpa. She didn't know why Gran thought the Wilders were responsible for Grandpa's death. Stacey only knew that to Gran, Grandpa's anonymity was vitally important and the Wilders weren't to be trusted.

"I can't say," she said in response to Ace Wilder's question.

"Can't?" Dane asked. "Or won't?"

She shook her head. "I was just doing a favor for someone, that's all."

"Come to think of it," Ace said, "you are too young to be the one who's been coming all these years. You would have been a baby when he died, if you were even born yet."

"Who sent you?" Dane asked.

"Does it matter?" she asked.

"Not to me," Ace said. "Except that we'd really like to be able to put a name on the headstone. Nobody should have to spend eternity in an unmarked grave."

Again Stacey shook her head. "I'm sorry. I can't help you."

Ace took a sip of his coffee, then cocked his head. "Why Jim Beam?"

"I don't know," she told him. "I'm just the errand girl."

"A few times in the past we've found two sets of footprints. I assume you came along at those times?"

"Does it matter?"

"No." Ace shook his head. "I'm just curious. We've left letters before, to whoever was coming up there, inviting them to use the ranch road and drive to the cemetery, in the daylight, if they wanted, no questions asked."

"I don't know anything about that." And she didn't. But she would damn sure be asking Gran about it. Why all this cloak-and-dagger business, if the Wilders didn't care one way or the other?

The door of the outer office opened and Stacey heard the sergeant greet someone with enthusiasm and direct the person to the sheriff's office. A moment later a beautiful woman with black hair and blue eyes stepped into the doorway.

"Knock-knock?" She paused and looked expectantly at first Ace Wilder, then the sheriff. She wore rubber boots up to her knees, denim pants and a white smock that billowed out over her obvious pregnancy. "Am I interrupting?"

"Not at all." The sheriff rose to his feet with a huge smile. "Come on in. You're just in time. Rachel, meet Stacey Landers. Stacey, this is Rachel Lewis, the county's best veterinarian, and Ace's sister."

The last part of Dane's introduction was more than obvious. Rachel Lewis was a softer, feminine version of her older brother. Stacey reached for her crutches, intending to rise to greet the woman properly.

Rachel stepped forward with a smile and an extended hand. "Don't get up. I've been on crutches before. Getting up and down with them is not a bit easier than it is with this," she declared laughingly as she patted her belly.

Stacey accepted the woman's handshake. "Pleased to meet you."

Rachel eyed her brother, then the sheriff. "Well? Have you caught the rustlers yet?"

"We're working on it," Dane said.

"I can't believe they hit the Flying Ace." There was a fire in her eyes that boded no good if she ever got her hands on the cattle thieves. "Do you have any leads?"

"How about an eye witness who can identify two of them?" Ace said.

"No kidding? Who?"

Both men nodded toward Stacey, but Dane said,

"I'd like to keep Stacey's involvement quiet for the time being, so let's just keep this among ourselves for now."

"All right," Rachel said, her brow furrowed. "You really saw them?" she asked Stacey. "How? Where?"

"Actually," Ace said, "Stacey paid a visit to the ranch last night."

Rachel eyed her brother. "Why do you say that as though I'm supposed to be amazed? People do visit the ranch now and then."

"Yes, but Stacey didn't come to see us, she came to leave a bottle of Jim Beam at the stranger's grave."

Rachel's eyes widened and her mouth fell open. She stared at Stacey for a long minute, then let out a cheer. "Finally! Maybe now we can put a name on that poor man's headstone. Who is he, your father? An uncle? Grandfather? Do you know what he was doing here when he died?"

Stacey held up a hand to halt the enthusiastic flow of questions. She was more than a little surprised by Rachel's attitude, and Ace's, as well. She would have expected anger, maybe suspicion. Not this…this feeling of welcome, as though she were a long-lost relative.

"I'm sorry," she said. "I was only doing a favor for a friend. I don't have any answers to your questions."

Rachel's face fell. "Well, damn. I thought we were finally going to be able to solve the mystery once and for all. But your friend would know, right?"

Stacey shook her head. "I don't know. I'm sorry."

"But—"

"Come on." Ace interrupted by getting to his feet. "I assume you came to give me a ride home?"

"I did, but now that Stacey—oh, good heavens. You came to visit the grave and ran into the rustlers? You must have been terrified."

"She didn't know they were rustlers when she saw them," Ace said. "Come on. Stacey's got business to take care of with Dane, and I've got work to do at home."

"Well," Rachel said as Ace steered her out the door. "I hope we get another chance to talk before you leave town," she said to Stacey. "And I hope you catch those rotten bast—"

"Watch your language," Ace said tersely, giving the back of her neck what was obviously an affectionate squeeze. "You shouldn't cuss in front of the baby."

"Oh, very funny, Uncle Ace."

The two of them continued to bicker with each other all the way across the main office and out the door.

The silence left in their wake made Stacey want to fidget. She resisted the urge, but barely. What she really wanted to do was take another one of those pain pills and sleep for about twenty-four hours.

She forced herself to look at the sheriff. "What now?"

"Now," he said, "you look through some photos and see if you spot the two men you said you would recognize."

Stacey nearly groaned.

"Then we find you a place to get some decent sleep. You look like you're about to drop."

"Why, Sheriff, you say the sweetest things."

## Chapter Five

Stacey stared at one mug shot after another until she was afraid she would dream of all those beady-eyed men the next time she slept. Which, thank God, would be soon, now that she had finished that little task and come up empty.

A few minutes later the sheriff drove her to the local motel.

Stacey stared at the sign outside the motel office. "It doesn't really say that. Tell me it doesn't really say that."

Dane chuckled. "Are you making fun of one of our local establishments?"

"'We hope you spring on in to the Hope Springs Inn'? I wouldn't dream of making fun of something someone obviously put so much thought into."

"That's good." He killed the engine. "Because

we only have one other motel in town, and it's the Dew Drop Inn.''

Stacey opened her mouth, then shut it, deciding that whatever she might say would come out sounding just a tad condescending. And really, she didn't mean to poke fun. But dammit, it was funny.

He got out of the Blazer and came around to her side and helped her out. It was a longer step down than she had yet learned to manage on one leg and crutches, so she appreciated his courtesy. And she didn't mind the feel of his hands on her, either, but that would be her little secret.

''Thank you, Sheriff.'' *For more than just helping me down.*

''You're welcome. But I've changed my mind. You can call me Dane.''

Now why, she wondered, did her heart give a little leap at his offer? ''Does this mean you've decided I'm not a hardened criminal?''

''It means you put a little bite to the word *sheriff* that I don't entirely like. I'm hoping you'll go easier with my name.''

Unless Stacey entirely misread him, this was quite possibly an offer of…friendship? At the least, a cessation of hostilities. Not that either of them had been particularly hostile, but could this be a peace offering?

She gave herself a mental shake and headed toward the office of the motel. There was no need to worry about friendship with him. Their connection was strictly business. Law enforcement business.

Well, except for the fact that she happened to know his mouth tasted like warm honey and she liked the way his hands fit around her waist.

By the time she had her session with the sketch artist, her ankle would be well enough that she could drive, and she would go home. She would never see Dane Powell again.

If that thought left a little hollow spot just beneath her breastbone, it was probably only because she was getting hungry again. But she needed sleep more than she wanted food—and a shower more than any-thing—so, with Dane carrying her small overnight bag he'd retrieved from the trunk of her car, she sprang on in, more or less, to the office of the Hope Springs Inn.

After she registered, Dane walked with her to her room, the third one from the far end of the motel. She unlocked the door, then balanced herself on her crutches and took her overnighter from him.

"Thank you," she said.

"For what?"

"For carrying my bag."

"You're welcome. I'll call you this evening to see how you're doing."

"You don't have to do that." But for some reason, she hoped he would.

"Maybe not," he said, "but you'll be hungry after you've rested up, and the four blocks to the café is a long way to go on crutches."

"I'm sure I can manage."

"Probably," he told her, stepping back from the door with a small smile. "But I'll call you anyway. If you need anything, call the front desk, or my of-fice." He dug a business card from his pocket and handed it to her.

"All right," she said, taking the card from him. "Thanks."

She stood in the door and watched him walk back to his vehicle, oddly reluctant to turn away. But when he looked back, she fumbled with her crutches until she had room to shut the door, and closed herself into the quiet room.

Dane waited until Stacey closed the door of her motel room before backing out of his parking spot.

At least now he knew what she'd been doing out on the Flying Ace last night. That answer, however, sparked even more questions. Such as the name of the man in the grave, and why she wouldn't reveal it.

But that wasn't really a matter for the law. The Wilders had told him in the past that they would rather handle the mystery—and any answers that came their way—themselves. Still, Dane would like to be able to help them put a name to the stranger in their cemetery if he could.

Just now, however, he—and the Wilders—had more pressing business, namely the theft of approximately fifty head of cattle. Stacey was at the center of that situation, too, and the theft of fifty head of cattle was most definitely a matter for the law.

He had deputies on patrol, and he himself would hit the county roads later, after nightfall, but he didn't really expect the rustlers to strike there in the county again this soon, if at all. But before he went out again he needed a bed, a shower and a meal, in whatever order they decided to present themselves.

Since he made it all the way to his street at the north edge of town without a meal jumping out into the road, and since he wasn't in the mood to cook, his stomach was going to have to wait.

Besides, he'd told Stacey he would call her about getting something to eat later.

Now why, he wondered, did his pulse speed up at the thought of sharing a meal with her?

He could tell himself it was because he would be able to question her more about the men she saw at the Flying Ace. He needed more details about them, their truck, anything she could think of.

Yeah, he could tell himself that. And he'd be lying through his teeth. What he really wanted to do was stare into those blue eyes without having to think about rustlers or cattle or trucks.

No, what he really wanted to do was get his hands on her, but that was about as likely, to coin one of her phrases, as seeing pigs fly. Besides, he couldn't put the make on a witness, for crying out loud. How unethical was that? He'd already kissed her, even if she barely remembered it. He needed to back off and get a better hold on his professionalism.

He pulled into his driveway and heaved out a heavy breath. He would settle for staring into her eyes, but he doubted she'd stand for that for more than about two seconds. There was a brain behind those eyes, and a sharp one. One he itched to learn more about.

"Hell," he muttered as he locked his Blazer and made his way to the house. Now that he'd started thinking about those blue eyes of hers, and that tricky brain behind them, how was he supposed to relax enough to sleep?

Easy, he thought a few minutes later as he stripped and fell across his bed. All he had to do was remember that he hadn't had more than a short nap or two in the past couple of days. He was out before he knew it.

And dreaming of kissing her until she moaned in pleasure.

Some poor wild animal was caught in a trap and shrieking in pain, disturbing Stacey's sleep.

No, it wasn't an animal. Someone was blowing a shrill whistle in her ear.

No...no, it was...

Dammit, she didn't care what the blasted noise was, she just wanted it to go away.

But it didn't go away. It kept right on ringing and ringing and...

Ringing. It was the phone.

Cussing a blue streak, she fumbled in the dark for the phone on the nightstand beside the bed. "This better be good," she grumbled, her words slurred.

"I guess I woke you up."

Stacey groaned. "You oughta be a cop, Sheriff."

"Dane," he corrected.

"Ah, yes." She rolled onto her back and blinked at the ceiling. Or what she could see of it in the dark room. "My friend, Dane."

"I thought you might be awake and hungry by now. I can see I was wrong."

At the word *hungry* Stacey's stomach took notice and growled. Suddenly she was famished. "You weren't wrong," she told him.

"Hey, I'm a cop, remember? I can generally tell when somebody I'm talking to is half-asleep, and that slur in your voice is a sure clue."

"Okay, so I'm not exactly awake. That doesn't mean I'm not hungry."

"Well, unless you've figured out a way to eat in your sleep, you're going to have to make up your mind."

"If I say food, are you buying?"

"If I'm not mistaken, I bought your breakfast this morning."

"The county did, and thank you, but now we're talking about supper and I'm currently unemployed and have a hospital bill to pay."

"I'll buy your supper, and you can tell me why you're unemployed."

"That's none of your business."

"I'll give you a half hour to pull yourself together."

Pull herself together? "Copper, you have never met a more together woman than me."

He was chuckling as he hung up.

Stacey replaced the phone in the cradle and covered her cheeks with both hands. She couldn't believe she'd said such a thing to him. He was going to think she was flirting with him, for heaven's sake.

*Were you flirting with him?*

"Of course not."

*Are you sure about that?*

"Positive." She wouldn't. Not with a cop. Good grief.

But she hadn't lied to him. She was unemployed. And he was offering free food, which no unemployed person should ever turn down.

She tossed the covers aside and swung her legs over the edge of the bed. Only at the last instant did she remember that her right ankle wouldn't tolerate her putting any weight on it. Bending over, she felt along the floor and found her crutches.

Damn, she would be glad when she no longer needed them.

When she had shut herself in the motel room earlier in the day, she had felt so grimy from her trek the night before that she had stood on one leg in the shower like the proverbial pink flamingo that kept hanging around in her mind, and scrubbed herself from head to toe. Now she opted for a nice, hot soak. If the sheriff had to wait, so be it.

As it turned out, he did have to wait, but only for a few minutes, while she gave her hair a final pass with the curling iron. Sleeping on wet hair had destroyed any semblance of style she might ordinarily have. But she was never at her sharpest when she knew she looked like something the cat dragged in, so she took the extra time and let Dane wait. Around him, she preferred to have her wits about her.

Those wits nearly escaped her when she opened her door and found him leaning against the front fender of his Blazer, parked a mere four feet away. Why her heart should trip, she didn't know, since she couldn't really see that much of him. It was dark but for the parking lot lights. He was dressed as he had been the night before when she'd first seen him: boots and jeans, sheepskin jacket, and a cowboy hat pulled low over his brow. It was enough to make her mouth water, and she didn't know whether to laugh at herself or let the horror of finding herself attracted to a pushy, macho-jerk cop overtake her.

She decided on laughter, because if she couldn't laugh at herself, then what good was she?

"Evening, Sheriff."

His mouth was about the only part of his face she could see, the rest being in shadow, and its corners

quirked upward. He gave a slight nod in ac-
knowledgment of her reverting to calling him by his
title rather than his name. "Ms. Landers."

They might have stood there smirking at each
other all night—or at least until Stacey's stomach
growled, which it threatened to do at any moment—
but an icy gust of wind swept down the sidewalk and
snaked its way inside her unbuttoned coat.

Dane saw her shiver and straightened. He might
have needed that hard slap of Arctic air to remind
him that he was supposed to be acting like a sheriff
and not some gawking teenager suddenly facing the
prom queen, but she didn't. He rounded the hood of
his truck and opened the passenger door for her.
"Let's go eat."

If getting her into his truck meant he had to put
his hands on her to help her make the step up, well,
hell, the job ought to come with some perks, right?
He started to reach for her waist, but she stopped
him.

"Wait. Let me try it myself."

Dane frowned. He wondered if this was just her
independent streak or if she simply didn't want him
to touch her. "Are you sure?"

"Yes, but I expect you to catch me if I fall."

He gave a nod and stepped back. "Have at it, then.
Just do us both a favor and be careful, will you?"

"Why, Sheriff." She tossed him a cocky grin over
her shoulder as she turned into the open door of the
truck. "I didn't know you cared."

Oh, she was a pistol, she was. He raised both
hands in the air. "Just fulfilling my duty to protect
and serve."

"That's for city cops. I thought county sheriffs rode the range."

"Just get in the damn truck before you freeze to death and I lose my star witness and have to explain your corpse to the county coroner."

"Star witness," she scoffed. "I'm your only witness."

"True, so, yes, I'll catch you if you fall."

Stacey paused and gave him one more look over her shoulder. There had been laughter in his voice, but she had the feeling that he was, literally, a man of his word. If he said he would catch her, then he would catch her. She could trust this man with her safety, her life.

What an odd feeling, to know that someone would make such an offer, and mean it.

Not that she was planning on testing him. She had no intention of trusting her safety, much less her life, to this or any other man on earth. Stacey Landers took care of herself. Sort of, she thought, frowning down at her crutches.

But her need for them could be laid at Dane Powell's feet, so she figured he still owed her. She would simply do her best to make sure the need to collect never arose.

With her weight evenly balanced and her crutches spread wide, she swung forward, lifted her good foot, then stood one-legged and crouched on the running board.

"Good job," Dane said behind her.

Yes, she thought it was, but now how did she turn around and sit without dropping her crutches?

Dane settled the matter by steadying her with a

hand to the small of her back and taking the crutches from her.

The feel of his hand, even through her coat, sent warmth spreading through her blood, and she didn't like it. This ridiculous reaction she kept having toward him simply had to stop.

"I said I wanted to do this myself."

"And you did," he said, his voice sounding much too close for her comfort. "It's no crime to accept a little help now and then."

Sure, she thought, as long as a person didn't mind being let down.

But hadn't she just decided that Dane was a man who wouldn't let her down?

*What difference does it make? Just get in the damn truck.*

Right. And that's what she did, although in a manner that lacked more than a little in the grace department. At least she managed it on her own, more or less.

Dane shook his head and started to slide the crutches in behind her feet along the front of the seat.

"I'll take those, thank you." She practically snatched them from his hands.

He shook his head again and closed the door, wondering as he circled around to the driver's side just what made a woman so damn stubborn.

Harvey's Café was four blocks up Main Street from the motel. By the time Dane parked and they entered, most of the dinner crowd had thinned out, but the few customers there all seemed to know Dane. As he led the way across the room to the booth in the back corner, people called out greetings or simply nodded hello. Dane acknowledged each of them by name.

Stacey maneuvered herself into the booth and slid the crutches beneath the table, next to the wall. As soon as Dane removed his hat a waitress appeared bearing menus and tumblers of iced water.

"Evening, Sheriff." She spoke to Dane, but her gaze, alive with curiosity, was on Stacey.

"Marva," Dane acknowledged with a nod and a smile, ignoring the blatant question in her eyes. "Been busy tonight?"

Slowly the waitress pulled her gaze from Stacey. "Oh, about like usual?" Her tone rose in question as she flicked her gaze to Stacey, then back again.

"What's good tonight?" Dane asked.

Before Marva could answer, a bald-headed man approached. "Marva," he said.

"Hey, John, you back again?"

"I didn't get dessert," he told her with a wink. "Sheriff, mind if I join you?"

"Of course not."

"I bet you two are going to talk about those cattle rustlers that hit the Flying Ace last night," Marva said.

"Heard about that, did you?" Dane asked.

"It's all anybody's been able to talk about all day. Fifty head, I heard."

"Never was anything wrong with your hearing," John told her with a laugh.

"Okay, I get the hint," Marva said. "I'll go get you some water. Does anyone want coffee?"

They all did, so Marva said she'd be right back.

"John," Dane said, moving over and making

room for the man to sit next to him, "this is Stacey
Landers, from Cheyenne. Stacey, John Taylor."

Stacey eyed the man carefully as he slid in next
to Dane. Something was going on here, she could
feel it. John Taylor had cop with a capital *C* written
all over him. "Would that be Officer Taylor?"

Taylor's lips twitched. To Dane he said, "She's
good." To Stacey he said, "Detective Taylor, with
the Wyatt County Sheriff's Department."

Stacey shot Dane a narrow-eyed glare. "I've been
set up."

"What makes you say that?" Dane asked with
innocence that was obviously feigned.

"Because despite the mouth-watering aromas
coming from the kitchen," Stacey told him, "I definitely smell a rat. No offense, Detective."

"None taken," John said. "With instincts like
that, you should think about becoming a police officer yourself."

If she'd been wearing glasses, she would have
tilted them down and peered over the rims. "Bite
your tongue."

Next to John, Dane raised his brow. There was a
definite sparkle in his eyes, as if to say, "Be my
guest."

She tried to tell herself her cheeks were suddenly
hot because she still wore her coat inside the warm
café, but that didn't explain why her bones turned to
water at the look in his eyes.

"Stacey's not too fond of officers of the law,"
Dane said. "Although I can't imagine why."

"It could have something to do with how I ended
up on crutches," she said.

"No." Dane studied her with a thoughtful expression that made her want to squirm. "I think there's more to it than that."

"I don't know," John said with a wink for Stacey and a grin for Dane. "If you'd surprised me with a flashlight in the face and made me fall down an embankment and hurt myself, I might not feel too kindly toward you, either."

"How perceptive of you." Stacey rewarded John with a brilliant smile. "Now I see why you're the detective and he's just the one who got enough votes to get elected."

"Ah," Dane said to John. "She wants me."

"In your dreams, Sheriff," Stacey said with laughter. Good grief, she thought, she was flirting with him! She didn't flirt with men like Dane. She flirted with quiet, shy, *tame* men. Men she could handle. Men she could maneuver, and, yes, manipulate if need be. Men who wouldn't dream of telling her what to do. Men who always, *always* deferred to her wishes.

Dane Powell was a different breed of man altogether.

But a girl could dream, couldn't she? That didn't mean she necessarily wanted the dream to come true.

Marva returned then with their coffee. Dane and Stacey ordered dinner, while John asked for a piece of the lemon meringue pie he'd seen earlier in the pie case at the counter.

"Sure thing, sweetie," she told him. "I'll have your food out in a jiff."

When she left, they got down to business. John asked Stacey most of the same questions Dane had. Stacey told him everything she knew, except the identity of the man in the Wilders' cemetery.

"That has nothing to do with stolen cattle," she said.

"It has to do with establishing why you were at the scene," John said.

Stacey shook her head. "I was there to do a favor for a friend—the identity of whom is also irrelevant. You can ask until you're blue in the face, but I have nothing else to say on the subject. If you'd like to know what the cattle truck looked like, I'll tell you everything I remember."

John definitely wanted to know, as Dane hadn't asked her for any details. Stacey was happy to comply.

Once John had all the information he thought she could provide, including her brief description of the two heavyset men she thought were in charge of the operation, he finished his pie and told them goodnight.

"Is he as good at his job as he seems?" Stacey asked once she and Dane were alone again in the booth.

"I don't know how good he seems to you, but he's plenty good. Not much gets by John Taylor. I'm glad to have him."

Stacey cocked her head and studied him. "I think you mean that."

"Of course I do. Why wouldn't I?"

"Most cops I know would rather praise themselves than a fellow cop."

"You know a lot of cops, do you?"

"A few. I was married to one."

The fact that she had been married—he hadn't missed the past tense she'd used—reminded Dane how little he really knew about this woman. "Is that where you developed your low opinion of cops?"

"I don't dislike cops specifically. I dislike all kinds of pushy, take-charge, macho jerks. When they carry a gun, that just makes them..."

"Bigger jerks?"

"I was going to say pushier, but your way works."

Dane sat back and folded his arms across his chest. "So, you think I'm a jerk."

"I'm not sure. You're pushy," she said. "You're definitely a take-charge kind of guy."

"And macho?" He grinned.

"I'd say yes, but you'd take it as a compliment. As for you being a jerk, the jury's still out."

Marva brought the check and tried to entice them into ordering dessert, but they both declined.

"I need to hit the road," Dane told Stacey. "Come on. I'll take you back to the motel."

"You're working tonight?"

"That's right."

Stacey felt a mixture of relief and disappointment that their time together was ending. She had enjoyed their verbal exchanges. He kept her on her toes. She liked that.

But she liked a few too many other things about him, as well, so it was probably a good idea that they part company.

As they left the café people called out to Dane, as they had when he and Stacey had entered.

"Good luck, Sheriff."

"Yeah, catch those dad-blamed rustlers, will ya?"

"I'm working on it," Dane said.

"Be careful," another called out.

They liked him, Stacey realized. These people

genuinely liked and admired their sheriff. She hoped he realized how lucky he was. There were millions of people out there in the world who disliked cops of any kind, just on principle. Some of that dislike, she knew from her own exposure to several police officers during her marriage, was well earned. Perhaps Dane Powell was a different breed of cop.

But he was still pushy, he was still take charge. He was still macho. The only thing she wasn't so sure of anymore was whether or not he was a jerk. She would have to give that some thought. Maybe.

Or maybe, in the long run, it simply didn't matter. She'd be going home in a day or two and would never see him again.

And that would be fine, she told herself. She'd come way too close to the Wilders than was wise. Which reminded her...

"There's something I've been meaning to ask you," she said once they were on their way back to her motel.

"What's that?" Dane asked.

"Ace Wilder."

"What about him?"

"The two of you look so much alike, I was just wondering if you're related."

"We get that a lot," he said. "If you ever meet his brothers, Jack and Trey, you'll see that Ace and I don't really look all that much alike."

"Good God. You're kidding. Who in the world names their kids Ace, Jack and Trey?"

Dane smirked. "King Wilder."

"No way. Nobody would name a kid King."

"He might if he was Earl Wilder."

"You're making this up."

"Believe me, I couldn't. My imagination's not that good. And before you ask, I don't remember what Earl's father's name was, but he was a baron, from England."

Stacey laughed and shook her head. "That's outrageous. Doesn't the family produce any females?"

"Rachel. You met her today."

"And why isn't her name Queen?"

Dane chuckled. "The story I heard was that her mother put her foot down. But King and Betty Wilder compromised. Rachel is the name of the queen of diamonds."

"The queen of diamonds has a name?"

"All the face cards have names, but don't ask me what they are. Rachel's the only one I know."

"What a family."

"They're good people."

"You like them," she said. It was obvious to her by the tone in his voice.

"I like them. Sit tight and I'll give you a hand."

Stacey blinked. She'd been so fascinated by what to her was the weird naming of the Wilder children that she hadn't noticed they'd reached the motel. He'd parked directly in front of her room. She'd left the lamp on and could see the light seeping around the edges of the heavy curtains.

"Oh," she said. "I think I can manage."

Dane opened his door, then paused. "Ms. Landers, if you tumble out and land on your head I'm going to arrest you."

"On what charge, Sheriff?"

"Two charges—stubbornness and stupidity."

"Well. I guess you told me, didn't you."

She didn't hear whatever it was that he muttered

under his breath as he climbed out and swung his
door shut. She thought it was just as well. She
doubted she would have liked it.

Stacey swallowed her protest, secretly glad to have
his assistance when he helped her out of the truck.
Climbing down and out was definitely trickier than
up and in. Not to mention the secret pleasure of feeling his hands on her waist again. "Thank you," she
said, once she was firmly on the ground with her
crutches balancing her weight.

"You're welcome."

He followed her to the door of her room and
waited while she dug her key from her coat pocket.

"Thank you for dinner." She opened the door. "I
guess I'll see—" Her words ended on a sharp intake
of breath. Her heart whacked against her ribs and her
one good leg turned to water. "Dane?"

Her room had been torn to shreds. Literally.

## Chapter Six

From where Dane stood he couldn't see inside Stacey's room, but he could see Stacey. He saw the color drain from her face, saw her waver on her crutches. Instincts honed by years on the streets of L.A. went on full alert.

Drawing his weapon from the holster on his belt, he stepped into the room and around her, putting himself between her and whatever threat existed.

"Get out," he told her quietly. "Get in the truck and lock the doors."

"But—"

"Do it!" He didn't think whoever had trashed her room was still there. The only places to hide were under or behind the bed, or in the bathroom, and it was too quiet. No one else was breathing but Dane and Stacey, who was finally making her way out the door at his back.

The room had been nearly totaled. Only the curtains and carpet, from what he could see, had been left undamaged. Everything else from the bedding, the mattress, and Stacey's clothes, had been slashed or ripped.

This was no case of random vandalism—this was personal. Someone had either been really, really ticked, or they wanted to send Stacey a message she wouldn't forget.

The message, he noted, was scrawled in what looked to be lipstick across the dresser mirror. But before he moved in that direction to read it, he checked first to make certain Stacey was out and safe.

She was just climbing into his truck. He waited until he heard her shut the door, then checked beneath and behind the bed and in the bathroom. He'd been correct. The room was empty.

In the bathroom he found the underwear Stacey had evidently rinsed out and left to dry. It was now in shreds. Her makeup and personal products were smashed and in the toilet.

Yep. Personal.

He moved back to stand before the dresser and read the message—"You didn't see nothing. You can't identify nobody."

Oh, yeah, Dane thought. Real personal. The rustlers had just upped the ante, and Dane's blood chilled at the thought of what could and probably would have happened to Stacey if she'd been here when they had entered.

But Dane had a hunch they had deliberately waited for her to leave. That meant they probably knew she was with him.

But who knew about Stacey?

Hell, any one of a dozen or more people. From the original few, word had probably spread all over the county that the sheriff had an eyewitness who could identify the rustlers.

Damn. He holstered his weapon and went out to his truck. Stacey sat shivering in the front seat, but he didn't think it was from the temperature.

"I'm sorry, Stacey," he said gently. "That's not a sight anybody should have to see."

She swallowed hard. "What happens now?"

Dane sighed and reached for his radio. "Now we gather what evidence there is, and make sure you're safe from any more of this type of harassment."

"Harassment?" she cried. "Is that what you call it?"

Having no answer for her, he keyed his mic and told Dispatch to notify the city police of the incident and to send John Taylor and the nearest deputy to the Hope Springs Inn.

The Hope Springs Inn erupted with activity. Dane and his men ignored the onlookers who gathered to gawk at the sight of three county cruisers and two city police cars filling up the motel parking lot.

The first problem was one of jurisdiction, but Dane and the local police chief had always worked well together and made a special effort not to step on each other's toes. Technically the vandalizing of Stacey's room came under the city's jurisdiction. But because she was a witness to a crime under the sheriff's jurisdiction, and this business was directly related to that, the local police offered to help if needed, but otherwise stepped back and let Dane run the show.

Dane did use the help of the local cops. He had them go door to door at the motel and to the businesses across the street to see if anyone had heard or seen anything.

Dane personally questioned the desk clerk, who was also the owner of the motel. When he learned what had happened, the man was beside himself.

"Nothing like this has ever happened before," he said, bewildered.

"I know," Dane told him. Then he proceeded with his questions.

No one but the owner had been on duty since before Stacey checked in that afternoon, and no one had asked about her. The only strangers to enter the office had been the couple in room twelve, just down from Stacey's room. It had been a slow day.

In Stacey's room John inspected the damage, took photos and dusted for prints. He would have to take Stacey's fingerprints, along with those of the maid who'd cleaned the room.

There was no sign of forced entry. Had they had a key? A lock pick? The motel still used keys rather than the newer magnetic cards.

Just one more detail to ponder, Dane thought with disgust.

"Well," John said laconically, "at least we know the rustlers are close."

"Believe me," Dane said with feeling, "as much as I'd like to arrest them personally, if I found out in the next ten minutes that they were in China, I'd be a happy man."

"What?" The police chief chuckled. "And miss out on the glory of making the capture?"

"I'd be glad to let you have the glory," Dane said.

"I just want them arrested and put away. And they just upped the ante."

"You mean this?" the chief said, indicating the ransacked room.

"Yeah," Dane said grimly. "This. Stealing cattle's a felony, but it's generally not personal. This was personal, and I'll tell you, I don't like it, not one bit."

It proved impossible, even with all the law enforcement on hand from both the county and the city, to keep Stacey out of the room and away from the threat scrawled across the dresser mirror.

"I thought you were going to wait in the truck," Dane said, trying to steer her away from the dresser.

"I waited," she said. Finally she pulled her gaze from the mirror and looked at Dane. "How did they find me? And so fast?"

Dane shook his head. "It's a small town, Stacey. They must know someone around here, or they wouldn't have known where to hit the Flying Ace last night. Somebody probably said something to somebody else, and it just went from there. I'm sorry."

He was sorry, and he was angry. She was his witness, in his care, and someone had done this to her. He felt responsible, and there was no help for it.

"I'm going to make sure they don't get this close to you again, I promise." As soon as the word *promise* was out of his mouth, he wanted it back. He'd made a promise like that once before...

Stacey was shaking her head. "You can't guarantee something like that, Dane, and we both know it."

"Come back outside with me." He wanted to talk with her, but he didn't want everyone overhearing what he had to say, and there were plenty of ears to hear and tongues to wag in the tiny motel room and just outside the open door.

He steered her toward the Blazer. "Get in."

"I'm not going to sit out here by myself like a good little girl. Or like someone too silly to be let loose on her own."

Dane leaned close and lowered his voice. "I want to talk to you, and the truck is as private as we can get right now."

"Oh." Stacey felt foolish for her comment. He only wanted to talk to her. "Okay." She let him help her into the vehicle.

He circled the hood and climbed into the driver's seat. After starting the engine to get the heat running, he turned sideways and braced his arm on the back of her seat. "I'm going to call out to the Flying Ace. I want you to stay with the Wilders until—"

"No way. I'm not asking them for any favors. They have no reason to trust me. They're strangers, and that's the way I plan to keep it."

"Stacey, be reasonable," Dane said. "They'd love to have you stay with them so they can ask you about the grave, but you don't have to tell them anything. They'll respect your privacy, I swear. And no one can get to you out there."

Stacey shook her head again, more vehemently this time. She would not stay with the Wilders. Absolutely not. Not with what her grandmother suspected them of. "No," she said to Dane. "I won't go."

"I could always lock you up."

She narrowed her eyes and glared at him. "You could try, but it wouldn't be pretty."

"They call it protective custody. It's perfectly legal, and it's for your own safety."

"I know what it's called, and you can forget it, copper. I'm not staying with the Wilders, and I'm not staying in a damn cell."

"You're not staying on your own."

"I'll go home. They won't find me there."

Dane snorted. "They found your motel room without asking for directions. They know about you, they probably also know your name. It's a simple matter to find your address. Since the Internet, there's no such thing as privacy anymore."

The thought that they might find her at home threatened to unnerve her. "Great. That's just great."

"If you won't stay with the Wilders, there's only one other option left."

"Why do I have the feeling I'm not going to like this?" she demanded.

"You'll be staying with me."

Stacey paused. For a minute there she thought he'd said she would stay with him.

"I'm not letting you out of my sight until I can assure your safety."

Good God, he *had* said…"Define 'out of my sight.'"

"Just what it sounds like," Dane said. "Where I go, you go, and vice versa. If anyone wants to get to you, they'll have to go through me."

An icy shiver ran down Stacey's spine, just one of many that had chilled her to the bone since opening the door to her room more than an hour ago and finding it and everything in it destroyed. Right then she wanted nothing more than to curl up in Dane's arms, which was the one place on earth she instinctively knew she would be safe. He was a man to protect a woman.

But he wasn't offering to hold her. Only to stand between her and trouble, which was his job. "Do you really think it's necessary?"

Dane could see how scared she was and could have kicked himself for making it worse. He intended to keep her safe, but he didn't have to terrify her in the process. "Probably not, but wouldn't you rather be safe than sorry?"

"Do I have a choice?"

"No. You don't."

Dane might have said more, might have tried to make the situation sound more palatable, but John tapped on the hood of the Blazer to get his attention.

"Sit tight," Dane told Stacey. "I'll be right back."

With her arms wrapped around herself for warmth, Stacey watched Dane climb out and talk to John.

She felt helpless, as if her entire world were spinning out of control. And she felt frightened. She hadn't felt either, not seriously, since childhood, and she didn't care for them rearing their ugly little heads again.

As Dane spoke with John, Stacey watched the confident movement of Dane's hands, the almost arrogant tilt of his head. Here was a man not easily intimidated. She would go along with him, because she didn't see any viable option. She only wished that deep inside, behind the fear and helplessness, she didn't detect a slight stirring of...anticipation.

\* \* \*

They returned to the sheriff's office where Dane and John wrote up their reports. Too restless to sit, and fearing their paperwork might take a while, Stacey swallowed a couple of ibuprofen—she'd had enough of the prescription painkiller, thank you very much—and paced the main office.

There wasn't much to see other than desks and file cabinets, except for the snapshots and wanted posters on the walls. She studied the FBI's Ten Most Wanted list, deciding she didn't know any of the losers staring back at her.

There was a long line of framed photographs and citations on one wall. She decided to start with the oldest. It was easy to spot, as the sheriff and his deputies were on horseback.

On second thought, considering there had been a cattle rustling last night, Stacey decided that deputies on horseback did not necessarily mean the picture was from the distant past. It could have been taken yesterday.

But the photograph she was looking at was definitely old, if the hair and clothing styles were anything to go by, not to mention the muddy street lined with false-fronted buildings and the occasional tent.

The small brass plate read Wyatt County Sheriff Bass Rogers and his Deputies, September 12, 1887.

Each and every man in the shot looked, as Gran would say, tough enough to wrestle a grizzly and come out on top.

While Stacey admitted to having a negative attitude toward cops, it wasn't what they did for a living that irritated her, it was the type of man the job tended to draw. Not just the tough and the fair-minded, which the job needed, but the bullies, like her ex and his buddies, men who thought the gun on their belt made them bigger men, and they didn't mind acting like it.

However, despite her negative feelings, she acknowledged the need for men and women to step forward and stand between the honest citizens and those who would take advantage of them and do them harm. Some did it for the thrill, and it was those she detested. Others did it because it was their way of making a difference in the world. Those were the ones she admired.

Dane Powell, she decided, was one of the latter.

Stacey moved slowly down the line of photos, studying each one, noting the slight differences in clothes, hair and scenery as the years advanced. Trying to pick by appearances alone which men where the bullies, the thrill seekers, the do-gooders, and the ones just trying to make life better for the people in their community.

She was looking at the 1952 shot when Dane finished his paperwork and emerged from his office.

"Ready to hit the road, partner?" he asked.

Stacey rolled her eyes. "Are you going to deputize me, Sheriff? Do I get to wear a badge and carry a gun?"

Dane grinned from ear to ear. "In your dreams, Ms. Landers. In your dreams."

The night was dark and long as Dane and Stacey cruised the highways and back roads of Wyatt County. They rode in what turned out to be a comfortable silence for nearly an hour before Stacey spoke.

"Why do you do this?"

She'd been so quiet that Dane had nearly forgotten she was there in the seat beside him. Nearly, but not quite. "Do what, specifically?" The scent of her, something sweet and flowery, but soft and subtle, had been teasing him since he'd picked her up for dinner hours earlier. His Blazer, he feared, would never smell the same.

"Drive around in the middle of the night while everyone in the county is asleep," she said.

Dane shrugged. "So they can sleep without having to worry so much."

"Why not let your deputies do it?"

Now that she'd decided to talk, he almost wished she'd kept quiet. Her voice was too soft, too silky. Too intimate in the enclosed confines of the dark vehicle with nothing but the occasional crackle on the radio to break the silence.

"Yoo-hoo," she said. "Earth to Sheriff Powell."

"Sorry. I was thinking about something." And if he didn't stop thinking about it, about her, he was going to get himself in deep trouble. He'd do better to pay attention. "Why do I work all night?"

"Yes. It seems to me the sheriff would be needed in the office during the day."

"That's where I usually am. But with these rustlers running around, my undersheriff and I split the difference. He's manning the day shift and I'm prowling around at night."

"But you're the boss. Why not make him drive around all night?"

"Because he's got a wife and three little kids. There's no sense completely disrupting his family life when I can take this shift with no bother."

"Mr. Nice Guy, huh?"

"That's me."

"Did you grow up here?" she asked.

Dane slowed for the four-way stop ahead and glanced at her. "Are you writing a book?"

"I'm just curious," she said.

"And bored?"

"Sleepy."

With no traffic coming, he crossed the intersection to drive past several small farms. "You can sleep if you want," he offered.

"Maybe later. Did you grow up here?"

Dane chucked. "Persistent, aren't you? No, I moved here from California."

"That's a long way from Wyoming. How'd you end up sheriff of Wyatt County?"

"Like you said, I'm the guy who got the most votes."

"You don't like to talk about yourself much, do you?" she asked with a smile in her voice.

"About as much as you do," he said. "Except I generally tell the truth."

"You got me there."

"Okay, I answered your questions," he said. "Now it's your turn. What do you do in Cheyenne?"

"These days, not much."

"Earlier tonight you said you were unemployed. Is that by choice?"

"No, it's not. The company I worked for got bought up by a European conglomerate who moved our offices to their U.S. headquarters in New York. They didn't need another office manager, so I wasn't invited along for the move."

"That's tough," Dane said. "But I'd think a good office manager would be able to find a new job with-

out too much trouble. Heck, I'm looking for one myself right now. Wanna move to Hope Springs?''

She chuckled. ''You're assuming I'm a good office manager.''

''Aren't you?''

''As a matter of fact,'' she said, ''I am.''

They were quiet for a while. Dane glanced up the
driveway of every farm and ranch they passed, and
watched the fence lines for breaks. The chances of
his running across the rustlers in the act of stealing
cattle were slim to none, even if they did decide to
hit the county two nights in a row, which he seriously
doubted. He probably had a better chance of being
struck by lightning than spotting them tonight. And
there wasn't a cloud in the sky.

Eventually Stacey spoke, warming his blood with
her silky voice. ''You never did tell me how a California cop—you were a cop before you came here,
weren't you?''

''You still working on my biography?''

''Just answer the question, copper.''

''What was the question?''

''You could just tell me you don't want to talk.''

''I don't mind talking.''

''Just not about yourself, right?''

He didn't know why he was giving her the runa-
round. It was no secret what he did before he came
to Wyatt County. He guessed he just liked giving her
a hard time. He shrugged. ''I'm shy.''

She chuckled. ''Yeah, right. Okay, if you won't
tell me, I'll make something up. You ran away from
home at the age of fifteen and joined the circus, but
they made you clean up after the elephants, so you
quit and became a beach bum.''

"Where were you when I needed career guidance? I like your story better than the truth."

"Which is?"

"No big deal. I was a cop, in L.A."

"Aha. So you aren't just a politician."

"I'm not any kind of a politician," he protested.

"You had to be to get elected sheriff."

"Not when you run unopposed," he stated.

"So that's how you did it." She snickered.

"Does that lower your opinion of me?" he asked playfully. *Playfully?* When the hell had he become *playful,* Dane wondered, appalled. He had no business getting playful, flirting, teasing, whatever it was he was doing, with a woman under his protection.

"Do you care about my opinion of you?"

A woman under his protection who happened to be ten years younger than he. "I thought you were going to get some sleep."

Stacey laughed. "All right, all right, I give up. You just drive your dark, deserted roads and I'll keep quiet. I won't make you tell me you like me."

Dane didn't know what to say to that, so he said nothing. The next time he looked over at his passenger, her head was tilted at an odd angle in sleep.

She'd had a rough twenty-four-plus hours. Frankly he was surprised she'd managed to stay awake this long.

When he stopped for the stop sign where the county road met the state highway, she woke, but remained silent as Dane waited for a southbound car to go by. He would pull out behind it and head south himself for a few miles, then circle back north again and head for town. By the time they got back his shift would almost be up.

"Look at that," Stacey said, blinking. "Am I dreaming, or is that really another vehicle?"

"Hey, come on," Dane said. "We've passed other cars tonight."

"How many, two?"

"So this is the least populated area of the United States. We like it that way."

"I'm not complaining," Stacey said. "I'm just not used to driving for hours without seeing at least a few other vehicles."

"Well," Dane said as the car in question whizzed past the side road where he sat at the stop sign, "you're seeing one now." As the car sped on down the highway, Dane realized that it had no taillights and the light over the rear license plate was out. "And you're going to see this one up close in a few minutes," he added to Stacey.

"You mean we get some action? Are you going to haul him off to jail for no taillights?"

"You do have a real high opinion of cops, don't you." He might have taken real offense at her comments, but he could hear the laughter in her voice. She was trying to get a rise out of him.

"Are you going to drive fast enough to catch this guy, or are you just going to follow him all night? Where are your lights? Your siren?"

Dane flipped on the lights. "There, satisfied?" He hoped the guy would see the red-and-blue flashing lights in his rearview mirror and pull over without Dane having to chase him halfway to the state line.

"What about the siren? What kind of cop are you, anyway?"

"I think we can do without the siren for now."

But when the guy ahead did not slow down, Dane

sped up until he was less than a quarter mile behind him. The guy had to have seen the lights by now, even if he never looked directly into his rearview mirror.

Of course, with the taillights and tag light out, there was the real possibility that the idiot didn't even have a rearview mirror. The car looked like it was about on its last mile, with rust spots all over the trunk and back bumper, and part of the vinyl top torn and flapping in the wind.

But Dane could see an outside mirror on the driver's side, so the guy had to have seen Dane's flashing lights by now. While the fellow didn't speed up to get away, neither did he slow down.

"Okay," Dane said to Stacey. "Just for you." He hit the siren for a short blast.

The guy kept driving.

"Well, hell." Dane hit the siren again and let it go for several seconds, until the car in front of him began to slow.

"He's slowing down," Stacey said.

"You sound disappointed." Dane eased on the brake. "What did you want, a high-speed chase?"

"Nah," she answered. "I guess not. It would have been too boring. There's not so much as a curve in this road for miles and miles."

"I'm sorry your evening's entertainment isn't more exciting."

"Well," she said with a heavy sigh, "at least you tried, and for that I thank you."

As he slowed and followed the car off onto the shoulder, he shook his head at his companion and laughed. Then he picked up his mic and radioed in the tag number, which was now visible in Dane's headlights. It was a Colorado plate. Dane waited for his dispatcher to check the tag number and let him know if the vehicle was stolen, or if there were any outstanding warrants on the owner.

It didn't take long for the report to come back negative. The car was registered to a man in Boulder. Dane made note of the name while wishing for enough money in the budget to put laptop computers in all his vehicles.

"Sit tight," he told Stacey as he reached for the door handle. "I'll be right back."

"Do you have your gun?" she demanded. "Your handcuffs? Your billy club?"

"I have something even more powerful." He picked up his citation book and pulled the pen from its holder. "I have my pen."

"You're just going to write him a ticket?"

"If he's a good boy, I'll probably just give him a warning. From the looks of that car, I'd say he's got enough trouble already."

Laughing at her look of disappointment, Dane got out and cautiously approached the vehicle. He aimed his flashlight at the windows and found no one but the driver. At least, no one sitting up. These days a cop couldn't be too careful.

But something about the driver's head looked familiar, and when Dane stepped up to the window and the driver rolled it down and gave him a smirk, Dane bit back one curse, but let slip another. "Hell, Farley, what are you doing out here this time of night driving this bucket of bolts?"

Former Wyatt County Deputy Sheriff Farley James—"former" because Dane fired him shortly after getting elected—deepened his smirk. "Hell,

Dane, what's the great sheriff of Wyatt County doing out here at this time of night, period? You oughta be curled up in your bed, all snug and sure that the world is safe because you're in it."

Dane let the gibe slide. He and Farley had never gotten along. Dane's firing him only made their meetings more antagonistic.

"Whose car is this?" Dane asked, forgoing any more small talk. "And why are you driving it with no taillights or taglight?"

Farley swore. "It belongs to a friend of mine from Boulder. He got hurt on the job up near the Yellowstone. They had to medivac him out and he asked me to drive his car home for him. I didn't know about the taillights until it was too late tonight to do anything about them."

The story was plausible enough to Dane. Giving him a ticket might put a few dollars in the county coffers, but not enough to buy the next round of coffee.

Dane wrote him out a warning. When he tore off the driver's copy and handed it over, Farley snatched it with a sneer. "Gee, thanks, Sheriff. The roads will sure be safer now that you've given me this."

Dane closed his citation book and tucked the pen into its loop. "Just be glad you weren't speeding."

"I am, yes, sir, Sheriff, I surely am. Hey, by the way, who's that doll baby you got riding around with you tonight?"

"Good night, Farley."

"Why, Sheriff Powell," Farley called as Dane walked back toward the Blazer. "You wouldn't have an unauthorized female back there, would you? Gettin' a little nighttime benefits, if you know what I mean, on county time?''

The farther away Dane got, the farther Farley leaned out his window and the louder he yelled. ''Wait'll word gets around about this. The high-and-mighty Dane Powell, gettin' it on in the county cruiser, while he's out cruising. Ha!'' He laughed hard at his own joke.

Dane ground his teeth and got back into the Blazer.

''Well,'' Stacey said. ''It doesn't look like that went well. What was he yelling about?''

''You were right,'' Dane bit out. ''I should have used the gun. At the very least, the handcuffs. But what I really want to know is when somebody's going to start making police-issue gags for guys like him.''

Dane didn't trust Farley James as far as he could pick him up and throw him. Since Farley outweighed him by a good forty pounds, that wasn't saying much for Dane's trust.

It was petty of him, he knew—juvenile, even—but Dane followed the son of a bitch all the way to the county line, just to make sure he didn't turn off somewhere and make mischief.

At the county line Dane turned around and headed north again, toward town.

''Is it safe to talk now?'' Stacey asked.

Surprised by her question, Dane glanced over at her. ''Why wouldn't it be?''

''Oh, I don't know,'' she said lazily. ''Maybe because you've been chewing nails—and I don't mean fingernails—ever since you stopped that guy.''

''I have not,'' he protested.

"Sheriff, if you gripped that steering wheel any tighter, I don't know which would snap first, the steering wheel, or that jaw you've got clenched so hard your muscle is bulging."

Dane grinned and relaxed. "Been noticing my muscles?"

"In your dreams, copper."

Dane chuckled darkly, but he feared the joke would be on him before too many more hours passed. He would be taking Stacey home with him. She would sleep in his spare room. No woman had ever spent the night in his house. The fact that they would sleep in separate beds, separate rooms, wasn't going to make much difference to his dreams. He very much feared the woman next to him, with the golden hair of an angel and the sweet smell of heaven was going to have the starring role in them.

## Chapter Seven

By the time they made it back to Dane's office and he took care of some of the never-ending paperwork that went with his job, it was midmorning.

Stacey was groggy with fatigue. Staying up all night and sleeping only a few hours, she didn't know whether she was coming or going.

Which was probably the reason that Dane was showing her to the spare bedroom in his house before second thoughts about the arrangement threatened to strangle her.

"I can't stay here," she managed.

"Come again?"

"You heard me." She turned away from the neat but plain room before her, with its double bed, dresser and chest of drawers, and faced him.

"I know it's not fancy, but—"

"Don't be an ass," she said. "I mean I can't stay in your house."

He cocked his head and stared at her with those deep blue eyes that made her want to stare right back and forget to breathe. "And just why is that?" he asked.

*Well, first there are those deep blue eyes...* "You're the sheriff, for heaven's sake. What are your neighbors going to think? Or are you in the habit of bringing strange women home with you in broad daylight and not coming out again for hours?"

He smiled. "Are you worried about my reputation, or yours?"

"You're supposed to be setting an example for the rest of the community, aren't you?"

"And if everyone else gave shelter to someone in need? Gee, I see your point. It could be the downfall of civilization as we know it."

"Besides that," she said, ignoring his sarcasm, or attempt at humor, whichever it was, "I don't have any clothes."

He blinked. Once, very slowly. "Oh. Yeah. Right." He seemed to give himself a mental shake, then looked her up and down in a way that made her wonder if the clothes she was wearing had been torn to shreds along with the rest of her belongings, leaving her all but naked to his gaze.

It was not, to her everlasting amazement, an unpleasant feeling.

"I'll get you one of my T-shirts to sleep in. It ought to cover most of you."

"Something to sleep in is the least of my worries. I don't have a toothbrush, or deodorant, or clean underwear."

"If you'd said something earlier we could have stopped at the store and picked up a few things."

"I didn't think about it," she admitted.

"Well, come on, let's go shopping."

Stacey frowned. "Just like that?" Where was the argument, the note of derision in his voice, the whine that he was being inconvenienced? Maybe even the threat.

"Why not?" He seemed surprised that she'd asked. "You need stuff, don't you?"

She looked at him more closely.

Yep, he was still a man. No one had sneaked in and swapped him for a robot. Or a woman. Or a saint. But he sure wasn't acting like most of the men she'd known. And thank God for it. She didn't know how long this generous, cooperative attitude would last, but she meant to enjoy it while she could.

"Yes." She gave him a big smile. "I need stuff. And thank you for offering to take me to get it."

Within minutes they were back outside in Dane's Blazer and headed for town.

Now that she was awake and paying attention, Stacey could appreciate the quiet, tree-lined street where Dane lived. The houses were small and so were the yards, and there were sidewalks on both sides of the street. The occasional bicycle spoke of young families, but there were older people, too, as evidenced by the gray-haired man waxing his 1970s-era Mustang in his driveway. He waved as they drove past, and Dane returned the wave.

At the end of the street Dane sat at the stop sign and looked at her. "Where to first? Drugstore or clothes?"

She shrugged. "Drugstore, I guess."

"Drugstore, it is." He turned right and drove two blocks to Sumner's Drugstore. "I don't know how much you'll find that you're wanting at either store."

"I'll manage," she told him. She wasn't about to complain about lack of variety. She would be grateful to get the essentials. Like deodorant and some basic makeup.

Dane helped her out of the Blazer, then held the door of the drugstore open for her to enter. A bell overhead dinged.

"Come on in," a woman's voice called out from somewhere. "I'll be right with you."

"Take your time, Ida," Dane called back.

"That you, Sheriff?"

"That's me."

"Heard you had some excitement last night." The woman emerged from a doorway behind a genuine old-fashioned soda fountain. Her steel-gray hair and the lines on her face had Stacey guessing she was in her mid-seventies.

"Oh," the woman said when she spotted Stacey. "Hello, there."

"Stacey Landers," Dane said, "this is Ida Sumner, the owner of the store."

"How do you do?" Stacey said.

"I do pretty good for an old lady." Mrs. Sumner laughed at herself. Then she sobered. "You must be the poor thing all the excitement happened to over at the motel."

Stacey blinked. "I must?"

The woman smiled. "Small town. Word travels. Not too many new women in town on crutches, you poor thing, you. Heavens to Betsy, we're all just thankful you weren't there when those hoodlums broke into your room that way. You're going to catch them, aren't you?'' she demanded of Dane.

''I've got John Taylor working on it.''

''Fair enough, then,'' she said with a sharp nod. ''John's a good man. A good detective. If anyone can figure out who did that terrible thing, John will. Now, what can I do for the two of you?''

''I just need to pick up a few things,'' Stacey said.

The woman slapped a hand to her cheek. ''Heavens to Betsy, if those hoodlums destroyed everything you owned, like folks are saying, I'd say you do need a few things. Let's see what we can do for you, hon.''

In a matter of minutes Stacey had toothpaste, a toothbrush, dental floss—''Oh, hon, you've got to floss every day if you want to keep your teeth when you're my age. Believe me, false teeth are just awful. Every time I have to deal with them I wish somebody had made me floss.''—comb, brush, deodorant, the bare necessities of makeup, and a tube of lip balm. Other than the dental floss, the woman didn't try to talk Stacey into buying anything she didn't want. But Stacey was grateful for her suggestions or she wouldn't have remembered to get moisturizer.

Dane carried Stacey's purchases out to the Blazer and drove her down the street to Kandie's Kasuals, the only store in town that sold women's clothes, according to Dane.

''Unless you want overalls, in which case we can go to the feed store.''

''Thanks, but I'll pass. Kandie's Kasuals looks fine.'' They had a nice window display sporting a pretty wool dress and three different pants sets. Surely she'd be able to find something inside to wear.

And she did, right down to underwear. Kandie herself waited on her and helped her find everything she wanted. She made nearly as big a fuss over Stacey as Mrs. Sumner had at the drugstore.

"Is everyone in town so friendly and helpful?" Stacey asked once they were on their way back to Dane's. She stuck her right foot out and admired her new fuzzy pink house slipper that was keeping her otherwise shoeless foot toasty warm.

"Except for the ones who break into motel rooms and trash people's belongings," he said darkly.

"Don't spoil things by reminding me," she muttered. "I was having a good time."

"Sorry. Here we are." Instead of turning into his driveway, he pulled past it and backed in, as he'd done earlier.

Stacey didn't ask why. She'd been married to a cop. Many of them preferred to back in, so that if they had to leave in a hurry on a call, they could get out of the driveway faster.

On her way up the sidewalk a minute later, with Dane following behind with her purchases, Stacey laughed at herself. "And I was worried about what your neighbors might think about my staying at your house."

"Does this mean you're not worried now?"

"Apparently they don't have much left to speculate about," she said. "It seems everybody knows who I am and why I'm with you."

Dane shrugged as he unlocked the front door. "If you'd let me take you to stay with the Wilders, the way I wanted, no one would know where you were or what you're doing. You stay with me, you more or less become public property."

"Now you tell me." She thumped her way to the bedroom he'd assigned to her earlier.

"Stacey." Dane placed the shopping bags on the bed and turned to face her. "I'm a highly visible person in the community. In the whole county. If you're with me, people are going to see you. That might let the bad guys know exactly where you are, but it also lets all the good guys know, too."

"You mean your deputies."

"I mean everybody in town. We're a close community. We've got our share of people who wouldn't cross the street to give a dying man a drink of water, but we've got plenty of the other kind, too, people who look out for each other, who care what happens to their neighbors, and even to strangers. It's an added layer of protection for you. But if you'd rather not be in the spotlight that way, I can still make that call to the Flying Ace. You'll be just as safe there. Probably safer."

"What, and give up the excitement of last night's high-speed chase?" She shook her head and smiled. "I'll be fine. As long as you can put up with me, and I can put up with you, I'm staying in your house. Are you going to make a pass at me?" The instant the question was out, Stacey wanted to swallow her tongue. She couldn't believe she'd asked such a thing! Couldn't believe the answer she was more than half hoping for.

The shock on Dane's face was almost comical. Almost.

"Well," she said, wanting to feel relief, but not sure it was there. "I guess that answers that question. I can feel safe around you."

"Of course you can," he nearly bellowed. "Good

God, woman, you're only twenty-five years old. I'm old enough to be your...your older brother.''

Stunned by his outburst, Stacey gaped at him. Then she burst out laughing so hard she nearly lost her balance on her crutches.

Dane braced his hands on his hips and pursed his lips. When she finally wiped the tears from her face, he said, ''I'm glad you think my age is so funny.''

''Oh, Lord.'' She tried to catch her breath but kept breaking up. ''Ask a stupid question, right?''

''You think my answer—or my age—is stupid?''

She broke up again. ''I'm sorry. You're right. I shouldn't make fun of old people.''

''Oh, now *that's* funny.'' But he wasn't laughing.

''Yes,'' she said, striving for some semblance of dignity. ''I thought so. Now get out of here, grandpa, so we can both get some sleep.''

''Older brother,'' he practically growled.

''Hey, old is old. I'd offer you my crutches to help you get around, but a cane would probably serve you better.''

''You're enjoying yourself, aren't you?''

''Yes,'' she said, surprised. ''I am. Now, scoot. It's not appropriate for grandpa to watch me strip.''

His only answer was a grunt as he headed for the door. But he stopped short and turned back to her. ''How's your ankle?''

It was killing her. Or had been until he'd made her laugh and she'd forgotten about the pain. ''It'll be better when I lie down and prop it on a pillow.''

Dane frowned. ''Let's have a look.''

''It's nothing a little rest won't take care of.''

''Is it still swollen? When's the last time you put ice on it?''

She shrugged. "I don't remember."

He narrowed his eyes. "I do. The hospital." He turned toward the door again. "When I get back, have that foot propped up."

"I'll think about it," she muttered to his retreating back. She didn't like being told what to do, and that had been an order if she'd ever heard one. She might have searched for the energy to tell him off, if her ankle wasn't throbbing so badly. Wherever he'd gone, propping her foot up sounded good. She just wished he hadn't told her to do it.

But she wasn't going to sit on that bed and relax until she'd taken care of a few other needs first.

Digging through her new purchases, she pulled out the toothpaste, toothbrush, cleansing cream, and a few other items and put them all into one bag that she could carry and still manage her crutches, then made her way down the short hallway to the bathroom.

When Dane returned to her room with an ice pack for her ankle she was gone. It didn't take a detective to figure out where she went. He could hear the water running in the bathroom sink. He moved her shopping bags from the bed to the dresser, then sat on the foot of the bed to wait.

He hadn't been sitting there more than a minute when he heard the water shut off. Then Stacey cried out. As if in sudden pain.

Dane was off the bed and at the closed bathroom door in two seconds flat. He gripped the doorknob but, at the sound of her swearing, stopped short of rushing in. "Stacey?"

The only response was more muttered curses.

"Stacey, talk to me." He had visions of her crumpled on the floor in a heap of pain and misery. "Stacey?"

"*What?*"

Okay, a heap of anger. "Are you all right?" he demanded.

"Oh, I'm just peachy." There was a definite snarl in her voice. And what sounded suspiciously like the pain he'd first imagined.

"You yelled," he said.

"There's that cop in you, noticing a little detail like that."

"How bad did you hurt yourself?"

"Bad enough," came her answer through the door. "But I guess I'll live."

Praying for patience—the woman was absolutely maddening when she wanted to be—Dane closed his eyes. "Do you need help?"

"No." Another muttered curse, "I can—" *umph* "—manage."

Dane paused, about to turn away and give her privacy, when she cried out again. Her cry was followed instantly by a crashing clatter.

"That cuts it." He opened the door. "What the— are you all right? What happened?" She was on the floor, on her hands and knees, between the sink and the toilet.

Her face, when she turned her head to glare at him, was beet-red from what appeared to be a combination of physical effort, embarrassment and plain old fury.

"I was trying to reach my crutches," she muttered through clenched teeth. The items in question lay scattered on the floor, one beneath the sink, the other next to Stacey. She lifted one hand and rubbed the top of her head. "One of them reached me, instead."

Dane was sincerely sorry she had hurt her ankle and then been conked in the head by her crutches, but he was hard-pressed not to laugh at the sight of her, mad enough to spit, with her rear in the air and her hair falling forward over her face.

If that wasn't enough to set him off, he'd just made out the pattern on her new white flannel pajamas. They were covered with dozens of little pictures of pigs with wings. Underneath each picture were the words *When Pigs Fly*.

Then he realized that he was staring at the part of her pajamas that covered her rear.

Fleetingly he wondered if all men were animalistic jerks. He'd never thought of himself in such terms, but what else could explain the fact that she was injured, partially because of him, she was a guest in his home, a witness in his care, *ten years younger than he was,* and there he stood, like some sex-starved letch, staring at her backside, wishing his hand was cupped there so he could learn if she was firm or soft, or that tantalizing combination of both that some women managed.

He oughta be shot.

"Here, let me help you," he finally said.

He lifted her by the waist and sat her on the toilet lid, but instead of releasing her, he slid one arm beneath her knees, the other around her back, and carried her to the bedroom.

"I could have made it on my own," she mumbled.

"You're welcome." He placed her on the bed.

"Okay, okay, thank you. I appreciate the help."

"Then you're going to love this." He grabbed the extra pillow from beside her and gently placed it beneath her injured foot. "Let's have a look."

"Don't touch it," she said in a rush.

"I won't." He tugged slightly on the hem of her pajama leg to get a better view of the ankle. Her bare feet were delicate and shapely. The bright pink polish on her toenails should have looked frivolous, but instead looked sexy.

Ankle. He was supposed to be checking her ankle. When he did, he winced. "It's pretty swollen." Clear down past her anklebone.

"Well, it's swollen," she agreed. "I'd have to argue about the pretty."

At least she hadn't lost her sense of humor, he thought. Reaching across her legs, he retrieved the ice pack he'd left on the foot of the bed. "Let's try this." As gently as possible he eased the ice pack against the bandage wrapped around her ankle.

"It's cold."

"That's why they call it ice. Get some sleep," he told her. Dane straightened and looked at her. She looked pale and tired. Dark circles marred the perfection of her skin. He had the most inappropriate urge to reach out and touch that beautiful face, offer what comfort he could. Maybe ease down beside her and hold her while she slept.

*Yeah, right.*

Okay, so he'd rather do something other than sleep. But that would just stay his little secret. If he even hinted at his attraction to her, she'd be reading him that saying on her pajamas in a heartbeat.

*When pigs fly.*

Abruptly he turned away. "I'll come back and take this off in twenty minutes."

"Dane?"

He paused at the door and looked back. "Yeah?"

"Thank you." Her eyes drifted shut, as if her lids were too heavy to keep up.

"You're welcome."

But she was already asleep.

Dane hadn't slept more than two hours when the doorbell woke him. He rolled from the bed and reached for his jeans. Dammit, whoever it was might wake Stacey.

He'd gone back and removed the ice pack after twenty minutes, and she'd still been out like a light. He had eased the bedcovers from beneath her and pulled them over her. He'd thought he'd awakened her, but she had merely curled up in a ball on her side and snuggled deep into her pillow.

The urge to stay had been strong, and shocking. Hadn't he told himself—more than once—all the reasons why he had no business being attracted to her? She was a witness, ten years his junior, and in his protection. She was the last woman on earth he could allow himself to get involved with. The last woman for whom he should feel a growing fondness. He shouldn't enjoy her wit, her sense of humor, her loyalty to whoever sent her on her grave-decorating errand. He shouldn't like her smile or the way she smelled or that sassy mouth of hers. He was supposed to keep things between them strictly professional.

She hadn't helped anything by leaving her personal laundry in his bathroom. After getting her to bed he'd discovered a dainty pair of pink, lacy bikini panties hanging on the shower rod to dry, and next to them, a matching bra.

His bachelor home would never be the same. He

was tempted to grumble and gripe about it, but what the hell. What man didn't fantasize about women's lacy underwear now and then?

"Forget the damn underwear and get the door," he ordered himself.

Just as he reached the front door, the doorbell rang again. Biting back another curse, he checked the peephole. "Well, hell." This could be good, or it could be bad. The way his luck had been running lately, he wasn't holding out much hope for the former. He opened the door. "Aunt Karen."

Karen Atwater was Dane's mother's sister, and he loved her dearly. She was the only living member of his mother's family he had anything to do with. But she could be stubborn as a Kentucky mule on certain subjects, and it had been a while since she'd stuck her nose in his business. He had a sinking feeling, brought on by the light of battle in her eyes, that his luck had run out where she was concerned.

"Dane, sweetie." She was a small woman and he was a large man, but she could envelop him in a hug tight enough to squeeze the breath out of him.

"This is a surprise," he said once he'd gotten his breath back. She lived in Cheyenne. Hope Springs wasn't exactly a short drive for her.

"I was on my way to Jackson Hole and just couldn't drive through your county without saying hello." She slipped out of her coat and handed it to him, queen to peasant, although she didn't mean it that way. "I stopped at your office and they told me about that dreadful cattle rustling." She patted him on the arm. "I know you'll take care of it, sweetie. You're a wonderful sheriff. Don't you think you should put on a shirt?"

"Yes, ma'am." He was thirty-five years old, but when she got that slightly disapproving tone in her voice he suddenly felt like an eight-year-old who'd just been caught tracking mud across the clean kitchen floor. "I'll be right back."

He hung her coat on the coat tree beside the front door, then went to his room and put on a shirt.

Dammit, he was a grown man. If he wanted to walk around inside his own home without a shirt...

Who was he kidding? He wouldn't offend Aunt Karen for the world. Not over something so simple as the lack of a shirt.

When Dane's mother had turned up pregnant with him, and unmarried, her parents had callously tossed her out. If not for her older sister, Karen, Dane didn't know how his mother would have managed. All his life Aunt Karen had been there for them. Now, but for the grandparents he refused to speak to for their treatment of his mother, Karen was, for all practical purposes, the only family Dane had. If she wanted him to put on a shirt, he would put on a shirt.

While he was at it he decided to splash some cold water on his face. He figured he knew what subject Karen was going to bring up. It wouldn't pay him to be anything other than as alert as possible. But when he left the bathroom to rejoin his aunt in the living room, he carried with him the mental picture of pink lace underwear hanging on his shower rod.

In the living room, his aunt gave his shirt the once-over and smiled. "Thank you, sweetie. From what they said at your office, I guess maybe I woke you up."

"That's okay," he said. "If you'd driven through

town without stopping you would have hurt my feelings."

She stretched up on her tiptoes and kissed his cheek. "You say the sweetest things."

He offered her coffee, tea or a cola, but she declined.

"I really can't stay but a few minutes. I just wanted to see how you were doing and find out if you've talked to the Wilders yet."

*Bingo.* Dane heaved a sigh, but managed to avoid rolling his eyes. "You know better than that."

Her sigh was every bit as loud as his. "I can always hope, can't I? You simply cannot keep this secret any longer, Dane. You have to tell them who you are."

It wasn't even a new verse, Dane thought wearily. Just the same old refrain. "I don't have to tell them anything. They're getting along just fine without knowing their old man was an even bigger bastard than they think. Or, should I say, without knowing he sired at least one more bastard than they know about."

## Chapter Eight

In the first bedroom off the hall, Stacy stood at her door, stunned. She couldn't have heard right. She must have misunderstood.

She hadn't meant to eavesdrop. The doorbell had awakened her. Wondering if there was news about the sketch artist they were waiting for, or the cattle rustlers, she'd sat up and this time remembered not to put weight on her right foot when she stood.

It took a minute for her mind to clear. When it did, she noted that not only had Dane removed the ice pack as he'd promised, but he had tucked her in and retrieved her crutches from the bathroom. She must have fallen asleep the minute he left after putting the ice pack on her ankle. She didn't remember his leaving. What she did remember was the gentle touch of his fingers against her skin, the soothing coolness of the ice, the swift easing of pain.

The thought of his tucking her in, touching her while she slept unaware made her heart race, but not in fear. With the prospect of news about an end to her need for Dane's protection, she'd grabbed the crutches he'd left beside the bed and made her way to the door, which he'd left ajar. It was only three feet from there to the living room, so the voices carried. She thought she heard Dane and his aunt discussing the fact that Dane and the Wilders had...the same father?

Stacey clapped a hand over her mouth to keep from crying out in shock. Dane? A Wilder? She didn't want him to be a Wilder! Granted, she had liked the two Wilders she'd met, Ace and Rachel. But she liked Dane a great deal more, and if what her grandmother feared turned out to be true, Stacey didn't want him to be part of that family. The current generation might be all right, but their father...no, Stacey did not want to contemplate Dane Powell being the son of King Wilder. If what Gran suspected was true, Dane wouldn't want to contemplate it either.

What cop wanted to be the son of a murderer?

In the living room, Dane's aunt tsked. "There's no need to be crude," she said in response to his comment about the Wilders' father siring one more bastard than they knew about.

Dane did his best to swallow his frustration. "There's no need to have this conversation again," Dane answered as gently as he could. "Aunt Karen, I can't tell them. You know my mother made me promise I wouldn't."

"Dane, sweetie," Karen said equally gently.

"Your mother, bless her heart, has been dead for five years now."

Five years, and he still caught himself thinking, *I've got to call Mom and tell her*... "That doesn't mean I'm not still obligated to honor her wishes."

"She had her reasons for what she did," Karen said, "but you know I've never agreed with her on that. She was wrong to extract such a promise from you. You need family, Dane. *Your* family."

"You're my family, Aunt Karen. All the family I need."

"That's so sweet." She reached up and patted his cheek.

Dane bit back a smile. She was the only person alive who could do that and get away with it. Anyone else, he would have decked.

"But I won't live forever," she went on.

"Don't start that—"

"It's true. No one lives forever. Your mother should be reminder enough of that. You need more than just me. When are you going to stop distancing yourself from the comfort of family just because my parents have been..."

"I'd fill that blank in for you," Dane said, "but I'm trying not to be crude again."

"Yes, well."

"What makes you think the Wilders would accept me, anyway?" he asked. "You don't know them, Aunt Karen. They're a close family. They have each other. They don't need anyone else. Right now I have their friendship. I won't risk losing that."

"What makes you think you'll lose their friendship? If they're good people, as you've said they are, they'll accept you."

"It's too late, Aunt Karen," Dane said, trying to get her to see reason. "I've lived here and known them for more than two years now. If I was going to tell them, the time to do it would have been when I first came here."

Karen shook her head at him as if to say he was a lost cause. "If you weren't going to tell them you're their brother, why did you come here in the first place?"

"You know why."

"Yes," she said quietly. "Because of Susan."

Dane stiffened. "I came here because there was an opening for undersheriff and I thought it would be a good chance to meet the Wilders and see what kind of people they were."

Karen placed her hand on his arm. "I'm sorry, sweetie. I've upset you. I shouldn't have brought up Susan. I know that was a…a hard time for you."

"It's history, Aunt Karen. Let it go. I have."

"Have you, Dane? Have you really?"

Dane's shoulders lost their stiffness. What was the use in trying to fool her? Aunt Karen had always seen through him.

But some things were better left alone. He was as over what happened to Susan as he would ever get, so there was no point in discussing it. No point in even remembering it, except to avoid repeating that particular mistake again. That particular fatal mistake.

"I've taken up enough of your time," Karen said. "I need to get on the road again if I'm going to get to Jackson on time."

Dane mumbled something he hoped was suitable, but as much as he loved Karen, he was glad to see her go. He would cheer the day they had a conversation that did not include mention of the Wilders, or Susan.

He kissed his aunt goodbye and watched her walk down the sidewalk and climb into her gray sedan. When she backed out of the driveway and pulled away, he closed the door. He stood there for a long moment, trying to clear his mind of their conversation.

As he stood there staring at his closed front door, something changed in the room. A subtle shift in the air. Something. And he knew he was no longer alone.

*Stacey.*

He turned and found her in those crazy pajamas, balanced on her crutches in the doorway. Those little winged pigs made him want to smile, until he saw the look of ripe speculation on her face.

"Well, hell." He braced his hands on his hips and stared at her. "How much did you hear?"

Stacey had a short, hot debate with herself. She could deny hearing anything, but as Dane had pointed out on several occasions, she was a lousy liar. She could admit she'd heard everything and threaten to tell the Wilders what she knew unless Dane arranged for her to return home to Cheyenne, which was where she most wanted to be, but if he called her bluff she knew she couldn't go through with it. She'd seen the turmoil in his eyes just now. Was still seeing it.

She couldn't imagine what it must have been like for him growing up having never known his father, his half siblings. Stacey's own father had certainly been no prize, but at least he'd been there. And now

and then, he'd had his good moments. She had a few
memories that still warmed her heart.

"How much did you hear?" he asked again.

No, she couldn't use her newfound information
against him. He was devastated enough by his aunt's
visit as it was. But she wasn't sure she was up to
telling him the truth, that she'd heard everything. Or
rather, she wasn't sure she was up to the eruption
she was sure would occur when she told him the
truth.

Being on crutches, as she was, left her at a distinct
disadvantage to deal with a man's anger. Yet she'd
had so much practice in her life, with her father and
her ex, that unless she had totally misjudged Dane,
she should be able to cope.

She didn't think she had misjudged Dane. Not that
he didn't look like a man who could get physical
whenever he chose. He simply wasn't the bully she
had first thought. He might very well get angry, but
he wouldn't get physical. Not with her. Not with any
woman. Not in anger. He wasn't like her father. He
wasn't like her ex.

Carl had never hit her—he'd be dead if he had,
and she'd probably be in prison for manslaughter, at
the least—but he'd been known to throw things, to
browbeat, to purposely try to intimidate her. From
what she'd seen of Dane Powell, he was a different
type of man.

She gave him a careless shrug. "All of it."

"Well, hell."

That was it? she wondered, amazed. A simple
comment on an expelled breath? "It wasn't as if I
eavesdropped on purpose," she added, just in case.

"Wasn't it?"

Ah, a little anger surfacing there. "You left my door open," she told him. "The doorbell woke me. I couldn't help but overhear. But don't worry, Sheriff, your secret's safe with me."

Dane didn't seem to care much for the breezy way she said that. "Is it?"

"Of course." But maybe there was something she could get out of this. It was worth a try, she thought, since he'd taken everything so well. "You promise not to ask any more questions about the man in the grave or the person who sent me here, and I'll promise to forget everything I just heard."

He cocked his head and narrowed his eyes. After a long moment, he agreed. "Sounds like a deal to me. But I can't promise other people won't ask you those things."

"But not your deputies."

"No," he said. "I won't put anyone up to asking you. That's between you and the Wilders."

"Then so is your secret." Tucking her right crutch more firmly beneath her arm, she held out her hand. She'd been right. Dane was not like her father or Carl. "Shake?"

Slowly he crossed the room and stood before her. He studied her for so long, she started to feel like a bug under a microscope, but she wasn't afraid, didn't feel the need to brace herself for a verbal blow.

He seemed to come to a decision. "All right." He shook her hand.

Stacey felt the sudden jolt of electricity from her fingers clear to her toes, and at several...interesting places in between. She jerked slightly and released his hand. She couldn't bring herself to look in his face to see if he'd felt it too.

"Neither one of us got enough sleep," he said. "We could fix something to eat, then go back to bed, or sleep now and eat later. Your choice."

After the jolt she'd just experienced, Stacey felt the need to retreat and regroup, convince herself she'd only imagined that sharp, tingling awareness. "If it's all the same to you," she said, "I'd just as soon go back to sleep, and eat later."

"That's fine by me. By the way," he said, "do you cook?"

Ah, a subject she could handle easily. Stacey looked up at him and smirked. "Read my jammies, copper."

The next time Stacey woke it was to the sound of the shower running. Outside the bedroom window the daylight was fading rapidly. She'd slept for several hours this time and felt wonderful for it. Even her ankle had decided to give her a break in the pain department. It actually felt normal.

At that thought she tossed the covers aside and held her leg up in the waning light. Hallelujah, the swelling was going down! In fact, the ankle looked so good she decided to give it a careful try.

She swung her legs over the side of the bed, then leaned down and picked up her crutches. Using them to get herself up, she gingerly placed her right foot on the floor. A fraction at a time, she put weight on it.

Not bad, she thought after a couple of small tries. She certainly couldn't walk on it without her crutches, but she was able to put a little weight on it without undue pain.

With Dane in the shower, she made her way to

the kitchen, using both crutches but putting her right foot down and easing a little weight onto it with each step. By the time she made it to the kitchen she felt triumphant.

She opened the refrigerator and scoped out the possibilities for breakfast. Her stomach didn't care that it was suppertime; it had just awakened. That meant breakfast.

"Are pigs flying?" Dane asked from behind her in the doorway.

Stacey peered around at him. Damn, why did he have to look so good with his hair still damp like that and a crease from his pillow still marking his cheek? "Pardon?" After his tender care of her when he'd carried her to bed and put the ice pack on her ankle, then that sharp zap of...whatever, when they shook hands, she didn't need to see him looking so good, so open and approachable.

He arched a brow. "Have you decided to cook?"

"In your dreams, Sheriff," she said with a grin. "I'm just taking a peek."

Dane sauntered in and leaned a hip against the countertop next to the refrigerator. "See anything you like?"

*Yes.* But she tore her gaze from it—him—and turned back to look in the fridge once more. "I'm not a picky eater. Especially when someone else is doing the cooking."

"You're telling me the pigs aren't flying, huh?"

"We could always hit the café again," she suggested.

He shook his head. "I'd rather not have you out in such a public, visible place."

That fast, the warmth of sharing teasing banter

with him in his cozy kitchen turned to the chill of reality. The bad guys were after her, trying to prevent her from identifying them. "Oh."

"Hey," Dane said softly, placing a hand beside hers on the refrigerator door. "It's just a precaution. Ask anybody, they'll tell you I'm as bad as a little old lady when it comes to not taking chances."

Stacey laughed at both of them. At herself for letting his caution scare her, when it should have made her feel safe. At him for the whopper he'd undoubtedly just told. "Yeah," she said with a chuckle. "I bet."

"No, really," he said. "I look both ways before I cross the street, I unplug my computer—the one at home, anyway—during thunderstorms, and I always cook my bacon thoroughly."

That got another laugh out of her. "Talk, talk, talk." She reached into the refrigerator and pulled out a package. "Let's see some action with this bacon."

The next hour was one of the more enjoyable times Dane had experienced in recent memory. The enjoyment—the surprised pleasure—had started when he'd entered his kitchen and found a woman there. He couldn't remember the last time he'd had a woman in his kitchen. Not ever since he'd moved to Wyoming.

If he'd fantasized about waking up to find a beautiful, golden-haired woman in his kitchen, however, he doubted he would have been creative enough to have her wearing white flannel pajamas covered with improbably winged farm animals. But for this woman, they suited.

She kept him company while he fixed bacon and eggs, although she'd been appalled when she'd realized that the package she had handed him contained turkey bacon rather than regular.

"You've got to be kidding," she'd said. "Bacon is pork. Turkey is..."

"Yes?" he'd asked, amused.

"It's stuffed with dressing for Thanksgiving dinner. It's drumsticks and leftovers. It's deli sandwiches. It is not bacon."

"It's lean and has no nitrites, and far fewer calories."

"What is this?" she had demanded. "A macho, know-it-all, health-nut sheriff?"

Dane had playfully narrowed his eyes at her. "You've got something against clean arteries and living longer?"

She'd narrowed her eyes to match his. "What kind of eggs are those?"

"Okay, so I'm not a purist." That's when he had noticed that she was putting weight on her right foot. "Aren't you rushing that a bit?"

"I'm being careful."

"I hope so."

And he did hope so. He didn't like the thought of her in pain.

Nor did he like the thought of her in danger, but if not for the threat against her, he wouldn't have just spent one of the best hours of his life with her in his own kitchen. He wondered if his enjoyment of her company, under the circumstances, made him exactly what she'd called him that first night—a macho jerk. And he wondered if his feeling close to her, when he hadn't felt close, not really, to anyone in years, made him a fool.

"What's on tonight's agenda?" Stacey asked when they were ready to leave the house. It was seven o'clock, well past dark, and well past cold outside his warm, comfortable home, she realized when he opened the front door. "I don't suppose I could just stay here while you go do your sheriff stuff?" She couldn't keep the note of hope from her voice.

"I don't suppose," Dane said, looking out at his neighborhood.

Checking it out, Stacey silently amended. Looking around at the neighboring houses, some with porch lights on, some with them off. The nearby cars, some in driveways, some parked on the street. Checking out dark clumps of shrubbery, large-trunked trees, anything large enough to hide a man.

She'd been married to a cop. She knew when a man was in his cop mode, and this was it.

But apparently Dane saw nothing amiss, for he stepped outside and held the door open for her.

This, she silently acknowledged, was not the time for her to proceed slowly enough to put weight on her right foot. Besides, it was still swollen enough that a shoe was uncomfortable. She was wearing her new pink slipper on that foot and didn't want to get it dirty on the sidewalk.

Less than five minutes later they made their way into the sheriff's office at the courthouse. Stanley Bates was on again, as he'd been the night before, as night jailer and dispatcher. Bates gave Dane his usual "Howdy," and welcomed Stacey back.

"Damn," Dane muttered as he stepped into his office.

Stacey tried to peer around him. "What's wrong?"

He shook his head. "I should have had you pick up something to read earlier today while you were shopping. I've got some paperwork to take care of, and I want to read John's report from the rustling site this morning."

"Don't worry about me," she told him. "I'm sure I can find something to amuse me."

"That," he said with mocking severity, "does not ease my mind. You have a knack for getting yourself into trouble."

"I do not," she protested.

He splayed his fingers and started ticking them off. "You get hauled in for trespassing, sprain your ankle—"

"That was your fault."

"Witness a felony, have cattle rustlers after you." He looked at her. "Unauthorized use of the department's radio," he added with a frown. "Shall I go on?"

Stacey glared at him. "All right, Dr. Jekyll, what did you do with Mr. Hyde?"

"Come again?"

"I liked you better when you were out of uniform."

Bates, seated only a few feet away behind Stacey, tried, and failed, to stifle a snicker.

Dane ignored him and raised out his arms. "I'm still out of uniform."

Which was true. He wore his usual jeans and flannel shirt, topped off with his fleece-lined jacket. But before they'd left the house he had clipped his gun to his belt. That, Stacey thought, must be his trigger, if he needed one. No pun intended. "You know what I mean."

"No, but then that's nothing new," he answered. "I'll be at my desk. Try to stay out of trouble."

She made a face at him and turned around on her crutches. Bates pretended to go about his own paperwork, but his lips were twitching.

Stacey looked around the outer office for something that might occupy her mind while she waited for Dane. She spotted a desk in the front corner that had been cleared of everything except a monitor—turned on, with desktop icons covering the screen—a keyboard and a single yellow legal pad.

While all the other desks held stacks of paperwork, small framed photos of spouses, children, or pets, this one held none of those items. Remembering that Dane had said he was in need of a new office manager, Stacey assumed this had been the former manager's desk. She wouldn't feel quite so much like an intruder if she sat there, she decided, so she took a seat and leaned her crutches against the side of the desk.

She really didn't need anything to do. She was perfectly capable of enjoying a little down time. After all, it had certainly been an eventful couple of days. But that didn't stop her from glancing at the neat handwriting covering the top, and evidently several subsequent sheets, of the legal pad.

It was notes, an outline, really, of things the previous office manager felt needed to be tackled by her replacement. Suggestions for improvements that she'd never gotten around to implementing. Comments on their frustratingly limited budget and where to take shortcuts when necessary.

Stacey itched to add suggestions of her own to the notes. She was, after all, an office manager by trade. But this wasn't her office to manage, so she resisted the urge to hunt up an ink pen and get to work.

Dane was having trouble concentrating on the paperwork before him. He'd been having this same problem ever since one Stacey C. Landers, aka Carla Smith, first appeared in the beam of his flashlight.

Two days. Was that all it had been? It seemed incredible, impossible, that he hadn't known her for weeks. Months. How could he feel so comfortable around a woman that fast, feel as if he knew her nearly as well as he knew himself?

He shook his head and stared at the budget again. He hoped the sketch artist showed up soon. Of course, that wouldn't make Stacey any safer. The rustlers still knew who she was.

If circumstances were different, he would send her home to Cheyenne. She'd been right about the artist being able to get to her quicker and easier there, and they could immediately fax or e-mail him whatever they came up with.

But he'd also been right when he told her it would be little trouble for someone to find where she lived. Particularly someone who'd found her motel room a few short hours after she'd checked in.

And that bothered him. They'd either been watching his office and had seen him take her to the motel, or they had access to information that they shouldn't.

No, he couldn't send her home yet.

And if that made him feel more relieved than it

should, he'd just have to get over it. Never, never again would he allow himself to get involved with a witness under his protection.

Dammit, he thought, staring at the budget. There wasn't a penny more money there now than there had been an hour ago. And there wasn't a thing more he could do about his growing feelings for Stacey than he was already doing—namely, trying to ignore them.

He pushed away from his desk and went for a fresh cup of coffee.

She was standing before what he called the rogues gallery—the line of photos of past sheriffs' department personnel—leaning on one crutch, putting a slight amount of weight on her right foot. Anxious for it to heal enough so she could drive home, no doubt.

He took one step in her direction, then stopped. He'd come out here to get coffee and clear his mind. Of her. Cozying up beside her would be slightly more than self-defeating. He turned away and crossed the room to refill his coffee. She didn't seem to notice him.

He stopped and talked to Bates for a minute, then went back to his office. He barely had time to set his coffee down when Stacey shuffled in on her lone crutch.

"Find something interesting?" he asked, nodding to the picture she had evidently taken off the wall.

"Maybe." She stopped before his desk and placed the framed photograph down. "You're in this one. Who are the rest of them?"

There was a tightness in her voice he'd never heard before. "Why? What's wrong?"

She kept her gaze on the picture. "Who are all these people? When was it taken? Do they all still work here?"

"Stacey?" Dane tried to read her expression and couldn't, other than to note she was drawn tighter than he'd ever seen her.

"Just humor me, would you?" she asked, still without looking at him.

"All right." He turned the photograph so they could both see it. It was the regulation departmental photograph, the same as had been taken every year since the first sheriff was elected in Wyatt County more than a hundred and twenty years ago.

"This was taken right after I signed on as under-sheriff about two years ago." He started with the front row of people and named them all. "Several of them no longer work here."

"What about these two?" She pointed to Ed Wilson and Farley James. "Do they still work here?"

"No, they don't. Why do you ask? Do you know them?" Her ex-husband was a cop in Cheyenne. Farley had two brothers and a cousin on the force there. It was possible Stacey had met him at some time or other.

"We've never been introduced, but I've seen them."

"And?" There was more, he knew it. He wished she'd just spit it out.

She glanced over her shoulder as if to make certain no one was listening. Then she leaned forward and whispered harshly, "Two nights ago."

Dane straightened in his chair. "Come again?"

"At the Flying Ace ranch. Near sundown."

"What are you saying, Stacey?"

"I'm saying you can call off your sketch artist."

## Chapter Nine

Stacey's nerves were screaming. "What do you think I'm saying?" she hissed. "That's them!" She jabbed a finger at the two grinning faces in the photo. "I can only identify two of the rustlers, but the two I can identify are right here in this picture."

Dane's eyes narrowed. "How sure are you?"

"Positive."

He stared at the picture, but Stacey could tell he wasn't really seeing it.

"Well?" she demanded.

"Hold on. I'm thinking."

"*What* are you thinking? I just told you—"

"Wait. Sit down and take a load off that ankle. I'll be right back."

"Never mind my ankle—" But she was talking to herself, because he had already left the office.

She couldn't sit. She'd just seen the faces of two

cattle rustlers. The rats who had trashed her motel room and torn up her belongings. While the former was by far the bigger crime in the eyes of the law, the latter, for Stacey, was personal. They had threatened her, tried to intimidate her. She wanted the creeps behind bars. Why wasn't Dane doing something about it?

She limped her way to the door and looked out into the main office, but saw no sign of him. She limped across his office to the window beside his desk, but the view of the small parking lot lit in the pale glare of a street lamp was not enough to hold her attention. She turned, ready to go in search of Dane, and there he was. He stepped into his office and closed the door.

"Here." He turned the group picture facedown on his desk, then laid out six individual photos, all the same size. Four were of uniformed deputies, two of men in street clothes. All of the men were approximately the same age, with similar coloring. "Do any of these men look like the ones you saw?"

Stacey rolled her eyes. He thought she didn't know what she was doing. Okay, she would humor him. She knew he was only trying to make certain. "This one and this one," she said, tapping two photos.

Dane picked up those two and pursed his lips.

"What are you going to do?" she asked.

He was silent for a long moment, but when he finally spoke, it was more to himself than to her. "It makes sense. They know every road and cow path in the county. Sublette County, too, which is where they started their little enterprise."

Stacey couldn't keep quiet. "Why would two former deputies suddenly start stealing cattle?"

Dane's eyes narrowed. "Money. Mischief. Revenge. I fired them, so they'd be glad to do anything that makes me look bad, such as not being able to solve the case. And they've always had it in for the Wilders, so it makes sense they'd hit the Flying Ace."

"What about the other county? Practice?"

Dane shook his head. "After I fired them they tried to get on with the Sublette County sheriff."

"He wouldn't hire them?"

Dane let out a sarcastic chuckle. "He didn't need to check their references—I'd have given him an earful if he had. No, he's known them for years. He knows they're both a couple of bullies who like to throw their weight—and their badges—around. Damn."

"What?"

"You know that car I stopped last night, the one with no tail or tag lights?"

"What about it? You don't mean…"

"Farley James was driving it."

Stacey let out a swearword that had Dane raising his eyebrows. "On the other hand," he said, "it's a good thing I didn't send you home, the way you wanted me to."

"Why is that?"

"One of them's got two brothers and a cousin on the Cheyenne P.D. and the other's got a cousin on the highway patrol. They could have found you in a heartbeat. They probably already know where you live."

Stacey swallowed. "I think you're scaring me."

"Then maybe you'll listen this time when I tell

you that the safest place for you is at the Flying Ace until these two are in custody.''

"Then go out and arrest them," she cried.

"There's a little matter of evidence," he said. "Or lack thereof."

"Since when is an eyewitness not good enough?"

"Since it's one eyewitness who saw two men, at dusk, while she was trespassing on private property. Even if a judge would give me a warrant—which he wouldn't without something more to go on—I can guarantee you Ed and Farley will have airtight alibis."

"So, what? You just let them run around stealing more cattle while I stay hidden in your spare bedroom for the rest of my life?"

"Not that having you in my bedroom doesn't have a certain appeal," he said, then got a funny look on his face as if perhaps he shouldn't have said that.

But it was too late, the words were out. For a long minute Stacey forgot about rustlers and ranches and everything else.

Dane cleared his throat. "The thing is, Ed and Farley don't necessarily know you're all I've got. Maybe there's a way to make them think I have more. If I can do that they might trip themselves up and make a mistake. But first I have to put you someplace safe."

Someplace safe, she thought, away from him. Where she couldn't see him or talk to him or…oh, damn, she didn't want to be separated from him. Not yet. She wanted more time to get to know him, to hear him laugh, to watch him frown.

And she was a fool for wanting those things, had no business wanting them. Just because he wasn't a jerk and didn't have a nasty temper didn't mean he wasn't still an opinionated, macho know-it-all. He was a cop, after all. It was a job requirement.

Still she didn't want to be separated from him just yet, even if she could see the sense in it. But she would not, under any circumstances, put herself within the power of anyone named Wilder. "I told you before," she said heatedly, "I won't—"

"Stacey, there is no place safer than Ace Wilder's house. He's a nice man, an honorable man, with a wife, three young boys, and a housekeeper all to keep you company."

"I don't see why you'd think his place is so safe," she muttered. "He can't even keep his cattle from being stolen."

"His cattle," he said with narrowed eyes, "were out on the range, not in his house. Anyone coming to his house can be seen two miles away, at least. Dammit, Stacey, I wouldn't trust your safety to anyone else, not even my own deputies."

"Is it because he's your brother?"

Dane felt as if been sucker punched. He wasn't sure that his breath hadn't completely left his body. Damn her, she'd promised. "Who's the man in the grave? Who sent you here with that bottle of whiskey?"

"All right, you're right. I was out of line."

"Damn right you were."

"If you took me to the Wilders I'd be intruding on strangers."

Dane could understand her feeling that way, but there was something else going on in that head of hers. He could see it in her eyes. "Not," he said, "if they agreed to it. And they would."

"It's an unreasonable idea."

"It's not unreasonable at all. It's the only way to make sure that Ed and Farley can't get to you. Dammit, Stacey, I'm only trying to keep you safe."

"I'm safe with you."

"I thought you would be, but that was before I knew who we were dealing with. Your ordinary, run-of-the-mill cattle rustler probably wouldn't come after a witness who was in the company of the sheriff. But we're not dealing with ordinary, run-of-the-mill criminals on this one. The two men you identified are mean and vicious. Nothing is beyond them. Nothing. With me you'd be out in the open too much. A sitting duck. We might as well stand you out in the middle of Main Street and paint a target on your chest."

It wasn't his words that shook Stacey as much as the look in his eyes. How could she have been so wrong about him? She had thought a lot of tacky things about him that had, she'd decided, turned out to be false. But never in her wildest dreams had she expected to see fear in the eyes of this strong, competent man. The sense of loss that fell across her shoulders nearly devastated her. She had been building fantasies in her mind about him, and they were all wrong. He wasn't the man she had thought he was. And that hurt more than was reasonable.

And because it hurt, she lashed out. "If you're afraid they'll harm you to get to me, just say so." The instant the words were out, she wanted them back.

Dane reeled as if she'd struck him.

"I didn't meant that," she said in a rush. "Not

the way it sounded. It's natural to be afraid. It's what keeps us alive. I don't blame you, honest.''

Dane closed his eyes and forced a breath into his lungs. He should let her think just what she was thinking, that he was a coward. If she thought he was afraid, maybe she would agree to stay with Ace. But dammit, he wasn't afraid, not for himself, and it stung that she thought he would be.

The only alternative would be to tell her the truth. He wondered if that would be tantamount to placing a weapon—another weapon—in her hands. She would be able to use it against him, that was for certain. But his ego was bruised enough right now that he didn't care, as long as she would stop looking at him with that mixture of disappointment and pity.

He was good at his job, dammit. He didn't want anyone, much less a woman he was growing to like more than was wise, thinking otherwise.

''Yes,'' he told her. ''I'm afraid. I'm afraid that you're enough of a distraction to me that I'll miss something. That I'll move a fraction of a second too slow. That I'll be thinking about things I've got no call thinking about instead of concentrating on the business at hand.''

Eyes wide, Stacey stared at him. ''What…what are you saying?''

Dane heaved out a breath. ''I'm saying that if you were a hulking, three-hundred-pound farm boy with acne and body odor, I wouldn't think twice about personally protecting you.''

This time she stared at him so long Dane was tempted to fidget.

Finally she blinked. ''Body odor?''

If she teased him, Dane thought, he might just

choke her. He had to convince her she wasn't safe with him. Because she wasn't. Right now, in the situation in which she found herself, she was the embodiment of Dane's worst nightmare—that she would need him, and he would be too slow, too distracted by his growing attraction to her. And she would pay the price.

"It might be distracting," he said, "but at least I wouldn't keep turning toward you hoping to get another whiff."

She swallowed. "Are you saying...you like the way I smell?"

"I thought I was clear enough," he grumbled.

"Clear."

"What part don't you understand?"

She frowned and shook her head. "I don't think I understand any of it, except that you like the way I smell. Maybe."

"I like the way you smell. I like the way you laugh. I like the way the light touches your hair."

Stacey felt everything inside her go still. His name left her lips on a breath.

"When I'm around you I think more about all the things I like about you than I do about what I'm supposed to be thinking about."

His words made her go all soft and warm inside. Again she said his name. "Dane."

"Right now," he said, "I'm thinking I want to kiss you, when I should be figuring a way to catch Wilson and James."

Stacey's heart knocked against her ribs. Her palms grew damp. She opened her mouth to tell him that kissing her wouldn't be a good idea, for either of them. But what came out was, "Why don't you, then?"

"Why don't I what?" he asked quietly.

She swallowed hard. "Kiss me."

He moved in closer, lowered his voice. "I shouldn't."

"Why? I'm awake this time."

The blue of his eyes seemed to deepen. "It's not smart."

"Probably not," she managed. "Unless you just, you know, wanted to…get it out of your system. So you could concentrate on your job. After."

"Maybe," he said.

Stacey's pulse turned thready. If he didn't do something soon she thought she might scream.

But he merely continued to look at her, and she couldn't tell what he was thinking.

"You don't have to," she offered.

"Don't have to what?" But he looked as if his mind was on something other than what she'd said.

"Don't have to kiss me." Stacey hadn't dated much since her divorce, but with the men she had gone out with, if she had stood around waiting for some of them to make the first move, she might have stood around forever.

Dane had shown no evidence yet that he was even remotely shy, but he had been, at times, reserved. That was fine with Stacey. That he wasn't quite as pushy and take-charge as she had first thought was a point in his favor, as far as she was concerned.

She didn't mind, in this instance, being the one to take charge. After all, she'd done it before, hadn't she? In her sleep. This time she intended to stay awake and remember every second of the experience.

She pulled her crutch from beneath her arm and handed it to him. "Hold this. I'll do it."

He looked down at the crutch in his hand and frowned. "Do what?"

"The kissing." She slid her hands up over his shoulders and around his neck, pulling him closer, until she could feel his warm breath puff against her face. "Look on the bright side. With any luck at all," she said, leaning into him, her lips nearly touching his, "we'll both hate it."

Her fingers threaded themselves through his thick black hair without direction from her brain. With barely the slightest pressure from her hands, he lowered his head and met her halfway.

The first touch of lip upon lip was almost tentative, as they tested each other and themselves. Then Stacey pressed forward again, parting her lips slightly.

His lips were soft and hot and firm. Familiar. They parted readily against hers.

Somewhere behind her there came a clatter that she barely heard and belatedly recognized as the sound of her crutch hitting the floor. She knew he no longer held her crutch because she suddenly felt both his hands against her back, pulling her flush against his chest.

Then he took over the kiss and deepened it, taking, literally, her breath away.

Those tame men she'd been dating had not prepared her for kissing a man like Dane Powell. Neither did the hazy memory of their last kiss. It was much better when she was awake to enjoy it. Never had a man's kiss turned her knees to water, her blood molten. She moved against him, trying to get closer, closer, wanting more of his dark, dangerous taste.

For all its depth, for all the physical and emotional stirrings it brought her, the kiss ended much too soon. When Dane pulled his mouth from hers, a tiny sound of protest made its way from her throat.

She was astounded to realize how hard she was breathing. More astounded that Dane seemed to be suffering the same problem.

He rested his forehead against hers. "I think," he told her, "our luck just ran out."

A slow, predatory smile curved Stacey's mouth. "Liked it, did you?"

He raised his head, his lips twitching. "What do you think?"

"I think you're pretty good at this."

Dane thought about letting his ego swell but fought the urge. "You're not bad, yourself." As he realized what he'd just done, he sobered. "But it still wasn't smart."

"Oh, I don't know," she said with a smile.

Dane bent down, retrieved her crutch and gave it back to her. "It just proves my point that you're not safe with me."

"Excuse me?"

"Look at us," he said, his mood darkening by the minute. He wouldn't let himself think about that damn kiss, the way she'd tasted, so sweet and tempting on his tongue, the way she made his blood heat. He shook his head. "Standing here kissing in the middle of my office with all the blinds open."

For a minute she looked hurt, and he felt as if he'd just kicked a puppy. Then that smart-aleck smirk he knew so well settled on that otherwise angelic face.

"What's the matter, copper, worried about your reputation?"

"I'm worried more about your safety." He stepped around her and closed the blinds on both windows. "I should have done this the minute we got here. It was already dark outside. With the lights on in here, anybody who wants to can watch every move we make."

"So what?"

She wasn't getting what he was trying to avoid saying aloud. He stood before her and gripped her shoulders. "Dammit, Stacey, if they can see in here, and you're in here, they can take a shot at you."

She sucked in a sharp breath. Her eyes widened.

"Now have I got your attention?"

"I thought we were worried about cattle rustlers, not snipers."

He meant to squeeze her shoulders, but ended up caressing them. "Stacey, you have to let me take you to the Wilders'. I can't catch Wilson and James and protect you from them at the same time."

She shook her head. "Put me someplace else. Anyplace else."

"Why?" he demanded. "Why won't you agree to stay with the Wilders?"

"I won't feel safe with them." The words came as if against her will.

Dane frowned. "Because you don't know them?" He studied her and shook his head. Something was going on behind those eyes of hers. "No, it's more than that. What aren't you telling me?"

Stacey closed her eyes and forced a deep breath. *Gran, I'm sorry, but I have to tell him.* "I won't feel safe on the Flying Ace because the possibility exists that someone on that ranch killed my grandfather."

*"What?"* Dane stared at her, stunned.

"I think I want to sit down." She hobbled to the leather sofa, sat down and propped her foot up.

"That should have been my line." Dane turned one of the wing chairs around to face her and took a seat. "Your grandfather. Is he by any chance the man in the grave?"

Stacey still had her crutch in her hand and noticed she was gripping it so tightly that her knuckles were white. She forced herself to loosen her hold. "Yes."

"Why would you think someone on the Flying Ace killed him? You couldn't have been more than a baby when he was found."

She shook her head. "I wasn't born yet."

Dane leaned forward and braced his elbows on his knees. "Tell me, Stacey. Talk to me. Why do you think he was killed?"

"She's going to kill me," she muttered.

"Who's going to kill you?"

Stacey swore. She hadn't meant to say that out loud, but in the long run she supposed it didn't matter. "My grandmother. She's the one who sent me here. She's the one who's been coming all these years."

"Let me get this straight. Your grandmother knew her husband died and was buried on the Flying Ace and she never came forward to claim his body or let anyone know who he was?"

"When you put it that way, it doesn't sound very reasonable," she admitted.

"What other way should I put it?"

Stacey shook her head. "I don't know why she never came forward. There are a lot of things about this that I don't know, that she won't talk about. What I do know, what she has told me, is that according to her, my grandfather, as she put it, went off the deep end one day, started ranting and raving that the high-and-mighty Wilders had stolen the Flying Ace from one of his ancestors. His grandfather, maybe, or great-grandfather, I don't know which.''

Dane sat back, startled. ''The card game.''

''What?''

''The card game,'' Dane repeated. ''I told you about it. About how the first Wilder came to Wyoming and won the ranch in a card game. Legend has it that he bluffed. All he supposedly had in his hand was a single ace.''

''And the loser felt as if he'd been cheated.''

''Quite possibly. Probably.''

''Was he? Did the guy cheat?''

Dane shrugged. ''Who knows? But I doubt it, or that story about him having only one ace in his hand would never have gotten started. Evidently there were a number of witnesses to the game. Whatever, it sounds like your grandfather thought Wilder cheated.''

''That's right. Gran says he decided to come here and confront the Wilders about it. Had it in his head he was going to reclaim what was his. I told you he went off the deep end.''

''Sounds like it,'' Dane said. ''So what happened?''

Stacey shook her head. ''When he told Gran he was coming here, he walked out the door and that was the last time she ever saw him. She's afraid he came here and caused trouble and that maybe someone on the ranch—''

''You mean King Wilder.''

Stacey winced. Only a few hours ago she had

learned that King Wilder was Dane's father, and here she was, essentially accusing the man of killing her grandfather.

"Your grandmother thinks they killed him to what, shut him up?"

She shrugged. "Maybe."

Dane gnawed on the inside of his mouth. "It's possible that it happened that way. God knows, if even half of what I've heard about King Wilder is true, he wouldn't have stood by and let someone threaten what was his."

She looked at him carefully. "It doesn't bother you? That your father might have—"

"Let's call him the sperm donor. He was never a father to me. In fact, let's just call him King Wilder. That's all he is to me, Stacey, a name. He never knew I existed. Say what's on your mind."

She wondered if he really meant that, or if it was a line he'd been practicing over the years to convince himself that he didn't care about the man. Whatever, all she could go by was what he told her. "That's it. That's all I know."

"Why didn't your grandmother identify him? I'm told they sent his photo out all over the state looking for anyone who might have known him. For that matter, why didn't somebody else identify him? Someone must have known him."

"I don't know. Gran won't talk about that part at all. Except, I think they'd just moved to Wyoming from South Dakota, so maybe no one here knew him. And maybe, if she really thought the Wilders killed him, she might have been afraid to come forward. I just don't know."

"Well there's one thing I know," Dane said. He

stood and took her by the hand and pulled her to her
feet. "We can dig out the file and see what it says
about cause of death."

Startled, Stacey nearly stumbled. "The file? You
have a file?"

"I assume we do. It would have been handled by
the county sheriff. And if you've ever looked in our
file room next door, you know we never throw anything out."

The file room was next to Dane's office, through
another glass-fronted door opening off the main office. And file room was what it was. The room was
about the same size as Dane's office, but it was wall-
to-wall file cabinets and nothing else. Not even so
much as a chair.

"I guess this means the files aren't on computer,"
Stacey said.

"We've got them computerized for about the past
fifteen years, but that's it."

Stacey gave a delicate sniff of disapproval. "Your
office manager should have seen to it these files were
computerized."

"You want the job?"

She gave him a look from the corner of her eye.
"Pul-eeze."

Dane grinned. "I didn't think it would hurt to
ask."

"Sheriff," she said in a haughty tone, "if I took
the job, you wouldn't know what hit you. Everything
would be so organized, heaven would weep with
joy."

"Big talk, considering you don't want the job."

She moved farther into the room and tossed him

a look over her shoulder. "Kiss me again and maybe I'll change my mind."

"I kiss you again, *I'll* change *my* mind. You'd be too much of a distraction in the office. Now, what year did your grandfather die?"

Stacey sobered. "The year before I was born."

"So twenty-six years ago."

"Why, Sheriff, you've been paying attention."

"I should have brought you a chair," he said, distracted. "This could take a while. They're filed by case number, more or less chronologically, rather than by a name."

"You'd have to look under John Doe anyway. They never knew his name," she said quietly, thinking how sad that was.

Stacey lowered herself to the floor beside Dane. It wasn't the most graceful move she'd ever made, but she'd been standing around on one leg so long she was starting to feel like a crane. Not to mention that she was simply, irresistibly drawn to him.

It took Dane twenty minutes to find the file on the John Doe found dead on the Flying Ace in the middle of winter twenty-six years ago.

His intent was to glance through the file first, before letting Stacey see the contents, but she leaned forward and looked over his shoulder. He slapped the folder shut, but not in time. She got a full view of a glossy eight-by-ten of her grandfather lying dead in the snow.

She made a tiny sound of distress.

"I'm sorry." He turned to her. "I didn't mean for you to see that."

She shook her head and visibly steadied herself.

"No, it's all right. It just took me by surprise, that's all. May I?" She held out her hand for the file.

"Let's take it to my office and look through it together." No way was he going to let her see the information alone. The man might have died before she'd been born, but he was still her grandfather, and sometimes police reports could be brutally blunt.

They went back to Dane's office and settled side by side on the sofa. The information in the file was straightforward, once they deciphered the handwriting on the old forms. Stoney Hamilton, who was the Flying Ace foreman at that time, had discovered the body. He'd gone back to the house and called the sheriff, who drove out to investigate.

There hadn't been much to investigate. The temperature had been well below freezing and so was the victim.

The file included notes on all attempts at identification, as the body had no ID or any personal effects on it. Fingerprints turned up nothing. Broadcasting a drawing of him—they couldn't have used a photo of a dead man—hadn't helped, except to generate calls from the usual crazies. The notes were fairly comprehensive. It appeared as though the sheriff had done everything possible to identify the man. King Wilder had even offered a reward.

A separate note stated that King Wilder had been out of town for several days and only returned home a few hours after the body had been found.

"That pretty much douses your theory," Dane said.

"Hmm," was Stacey's only response. She was engrossed in the contents of the file. "Here it is."

"The coroner's report."

"It says he died of exposure," Stacey said. "That he'd probably died the afternoon before he was found."

"You okay?" Dane asked.

Stacey took a final look at the photo of her dead grandfather, then closed the file. "I don't know. I guess so."

She didn't look all right to Dane. She looked as sad as if she'd just waved goodbye to her best friend. He slipped his arm around her shoulders and pulled her to his side. "At least now you know what happened to him."

Stacey let him pull her close. She eased into his embrace and lay her head on his shoulder. "Yes. At least now I know."

They sat there for a long time, the only sounds those coming from the outer office as Bates answered the phone or responded to a radio call from one of the deputies out on patrol.

Finally Dane asked, "What was his name?"

"Conner," she said. "Ralph Conner."

"That's the name of the original owner of the ranch."

"I thought it might be."

"Is that what the *C* in Stacey C. Landers is for?"

Stacey smiled and straightened away from him. "You ought to be a cop. You guessed it in one."

"Well," he said, smiling, "it was either that or Carla."

She laughed. "My ex-husband's name is Carl Smith."

"Ah. You still think about him so much that when I asked you your name, his came to mind?"

"Ha. The only time I think about Carl Smith is

when I have indigestion. Because it reminds me of exactly how I felt the entire year we were married.''

Dane let out a low whistle. "An entire year, huh? And they say marriage doesn't last.''

"Wise guy. You ever been married?''

A shadow seemed to cross Dane's face. His eyes lost their focus. "No,'' he said. "No, I've never been married.''

"You want to talk about her?''

His gaze sharpened. "Her who?''

"The woman you didn't marry. Would that be Susan?''

He stiffened. "Where did— Oh. Aunt Karen mentioned her. You have good ears.''

"I told you I didn't eavesdrop on purpose. I couldn't help but hear. Who was she?'' she asked gently.

Dane shook his head and pushed himself up from the couch. He stood with his back to her for so long she feared she had offended him or made him angry. Then he let out a long breath and hung his head, as though in defeat.

And Dane did feel defeated. He didn't talk about Susan, not ever. Not to anyone. But it was because of what had happened with Susan that his palms turned to ice when he thought of having to protect Stacey while Wilson and James were still on the loose.

Maybe if the suspects were strangers and he didn't know how vicious they could be, or maybe if he could keep his mind on something other than kissing Stacey again the first chance he got, he might be able to get through this. But maybes didn't count in real life. So he would tell her. Tell her what a failure he was and what could happen to her in his care, and she would be only too glad to stay at the ranch for a few days.

"She's the reason," he said quietly, "that I want you to stay at the Flying Ace until our friendly local cattle rustlers are under lock and key."

"What do you mean?" Something was going on here, Stacey realized. Something that tore at Dane.

He turned to face her, and she almost wished he hadn't. She had thought to see pain or anguish in his eyes. Instead she saw nothing but a deadness that chilled her. "Dane?"

"I told you I worked homicide on the L.A.P.D."

"Yes." She nodded, not at all sure she wanted to hear this.

"Susan was a woman who witnessed a particularly brutal gang murder. Not your average drive-by shooting, but a kidnap and torture. She was our only witness, and I was assigned to protect her while they tracked down the killers she had IDed in a photo lineup."

"What—" Stacey had to stop and swallow. "What happened?"

The self-deprecating half smile, coupled with the dead look in his eyes, tied a knot in her stomach.

"She was...like no other woman I'd ever known."

"And you fell in love with her."

"Hard and fast," he said, his gaze focusing now somewhere in the past. Then he shook himself. "The short version is, I was so distracted by what I was feeling for her that I didn't pay close enough attention. I let down my guard. And I got her killed."

"Oh, Dane."

Now his gaze focused on her. ''I'm afraid I'm pretty much distracted the same way by you, and I'll be damned if I'll take the chance of letting you down the way I did her. I want you to stay at the Flying Ace, Stacey. Please.''

What was he saying? That he was falling for her, ''hard and fast,'' the way he had for Susan? Or was he simply afraid he wouldn't be able to protect her? Either way, there was only one answer she could give for his sake. ''All right, Dane. If they'll have me, I'll go.''

## Chapter Ten

As Dane had anticipated, when he called the ranch at sunup, Ace didn't hesitate to offer shelter and protection to Stacey.

"This is extremely generous of him," Stacey said as they headed out of town in the Blazer. After leaving the sheriff's office they had gone by Dane's house. Dane had loaned her a duffle bag, and she had packed enough clothes for a couple of days. That was all, he'd said, that it should take.

"Ace is a generous kind of guy," Dane said. "Besides, you're helping catch the men who stole his cattle. And when you tell him who's in that unmarked grave in his family cemetery, the whole clan will probably welcome you like a long-lost relative."

Stacey glanced over and was relieved to see him smiling again. "Speaking of long-lost Wilder relatives..."

"Looks like it's going to be a pretty day," Dane said.

"Come on, copper, I spilled my guts to you."

"And I returned the favor."

He meant Susan, who hadn't been part of their deal. He was comparing apples to oranges, but that was okay. Stacey wasn't going to bring up Susan again; it plainly hurt him too much.

Although she wished dearly for the nerve to ask him outright if he'd meant he was falling for her, or if she was merely a distraction.

*Forget it.* It shouldn't matter, couldn't matter. He was too strong-minded for her. Too take-charge. Too…much.

"If you really think they're going to welcome me like a long-lost relative, I don't understand why you think they wouldn't do the same with you. You really are a long-lost relative."

"Not gonna happen," Dane said. "So give it up." Then his eyes widened, and his head whipped around. "You won't tell them. By damn, you won't."

"Don't insult me. Of course I won't. But I think it's gonna cost you."

He cast her a leery look. "Cost me what?"

"Oh, I don't know, but rest assured, I'll think of something."

"That's a comfort."

They rode in silence for a few miles, until they saw an approaching vehicle that was weaving all over the road.

"Dane, look," Stacey warned.

"I see it. Damn, that looks like Rachel."

"Rachel, the pregnant lady vet who came to your

office? Ace's sister?'' *Your sister?* she wanted to say, but didn't.

The oncoming SUV swerved sharply onto the shoulder and came to an abrupt halt.

''That's her,'' Dane said grimly. ''And something's wrong.'' He slowed down and pulled across the road, coming to a stop nose to nose with Rachel's Standing Elk Veterinary Clinic vehicle.

In the SUV, Rachel Wilder Lewis sat pushing herself back into her seat, her arms outstretched, knuckles white around the steering wheel. Her eyes were closed, her head was back, and her cheeks were pumping breath like a bellows through her open mouth.

''Is she in labor?'' Stacey asked as Dane put his vehicle in Park. ''When is she due?''

''She's not due for another couple of weeks,'' he said. ''But unless I miss my guess, nobody told the baby.'' He threw open his door and rushed to the passenger door of Rachel's truck only to find it locked. As Stacey made her clumsy way out of his Blazer, he rounded to Rachel's door.

''Rachel?'' He tried the door and found it locked, so he tapped on her window. ''Rachel, hon?''

She opened her eyes and nodded, but kept up her panting and retained her grip on the steering wheel for several seconds that to Dane felt like a lifetime. If ever he'd seen a woman in labor—and he had, more than once—this was it. But this was the first time it had ever scared him clear down to his bones.

Yeah, sure, he'd been scared the first time he'd had to help deliver a baby, back in L.A. in the back seat of his patrol unit when he'd been a rookie street cop right out of the academy. But that woman had been a stranger. This one… God, this one was a close friend, one of the first friends he'd made in Wyatt County, and, even though she didn't know it, she was his baby sister. Seeing what she was going through and knowing what she had yet to endure made cold sweat pop out along his spine.

But he couldn't let her know. To her he was just a friend. A good one, but nothing more. And he was the sheriff. She would expect him to be cool and competent, so that's what he would be.

Steadying himself became imminently easier when Stacey joined him beside the truck.

"Looks like the baby has decided to come early," Stacey said.

"Looks like."

"What are you going to do?"

"Whatever needs doing," he said. "Rachel? Can you unlock the door?"

Finally Rachel's breathing slowed and she relaxed somewhat and opened the door. "Boy," she said, "am I glad to see you."

"I guess we need to get you to the hospital, huh?" Dane said, trying to instill confidence with his smile.

"But it's too early," she protested.

"It didn't look like it from where I've been standing," he said.

"I tried to call Grady but couldn't reach him. I had an early call and was on my way back to the clinic, and— Oh, God, here comes another one."

"Breathe," Dane told her. "Little pants, just like you were doing. Everything's going to be fine, hon." His mind raced. He needed to get her to the hospital. A glance into her back seat told him she couldn't ride there. It was filled with veterinary supplies and equipment, as was the cargo area behind the seat.

He turned to Stacey. "Go make sure my back seat is clear."

"Sure. Anything else?"

"There should be a blanket in the back. See if you can find it." He turned back to Rachel in time to see her relax again.

Relax, hell, she nearly collapsed in relief as the pain eased.

"I'm going to carry you to my car and take you to the hospital. Okay?"

Rachel huffed out a breath. "Yeah. Okay. Thanks. And Dane?"

"What is it, hon?"

"Will you try to find Grady?"

"You know I will." When a woman went through this, her man should be at her side, Dane thought.

In between her pains he carried her to his Blazer, but she refused to lie down.

"I'd rather sit up," she insisted.

"All right. But the back seat is safer, and there's more room. You won't have to share space with my radio and shotgun."

They got her situated and buckled in. Dane went back to pull her vehicle farther off the pavement, then he locked it and returned.

On the way to the hospital he radioed his dispatcher and gave instructions that he was to track down Grady Lewis pronto, and call out to the Flying Ace and let them know Rachel was in labor. "And call the hospital to let them know we're coming."

Twice on the drive back to town they came upon

a slow-moving vehicle in the lane ahead of them. Dane flipped on his lights and siren and passed them.

Stacey marveled at Dane's calmness. After all, that was his little sister in the back seat.

Then she noticed how tightly he was gripping the steering wheel—almost as tightly as Rachel had been gripping hers in the throes of labor pains. And his eyes, when he glanced up and tilted the rearview mirror to check on Rachel in the back seat, were anything but calm for a second or two, before he reined in his feelings.

"How are you doing back there?" he asked Rachel.

"Okay," she said. But her voice sounded strained. "I can't tell you how glad I am that you two came along when you did. If I'd had to pull over every time a pain hit, the kid would be out of diapers before I made it to the hospital."

Dane chuckled, and so did Stacey.

"Do you know if it's a boy or a girl?" Stacey asked. It was what everyone always asked of expectant mothers. Stacey didn't see what difference it made. Boy or girl, a baby was a gift from God. But some couples wanted to know ahead of time, and with today's technology it was simple to find out.

From the back seat, Rachel said, "No. We decided we wanted to be surprised."

"Ah, you're doing it the old-fashioned way," Stacey said.

"Don't even say that," Dane said darkly. "She nearly got a little too old-fashioned and had it on the side of the road."

"Aw," Rachel said. "How sweet. He's worried about me. Thank you, Dane. I love you, too."

For the next five miles all three of them simply grinned.

When they reached the hospital, Dane scooped Rachel out of the back seat and placed her gently in the wheelchair a nurse had on hand.

"We heard you were coming," the nurse said. "Sheriff, you're starting to make a habit out of this. The doctor's waiting to check you over, Mrs. Lewis. Oh, sorry, make that Dr. Lewis."

"How about Rachel?" Rachel suggested.

After telling Dane that she would let him know what was happening as soon as she could, the nurse whisked Rachel away through a set of swinging double doors.

"Now what?" Stacey asked. "We're not going to just leave her here, are we?"

"We'll wait until some of the family shows up," Dane said.

The hospital was small. There was only one waiting area, and it was just around the corner from the main entrance. Stacey took a seat there on one of the two sofas. Dane paced the length of the room and back, muttering dire repercussions on the head of one Grady Lewis, Rachel's husband, if he didn't get his butt to the hospital soon.

Halfway through what Stacey estimated was Dane's tenth pass across the room, hurried footsteps approached from the hall.

"Dane?"

From the look on the newcomer's face and in his eyes, Stacey had to guess that this was the errant Grady Lewis. He was a tall man, as tall as Dane, but leaner. His shoulder-length hair was so thick and black that it seemed to soak up all the light in the room. His high, proud cheekbones and bronze skin spoke of American Indian heritage.

"Grady," Dane said with relief, confirming Stacey's guess.

"What happened?" Grady demanded. "Where's Rachel?"

Dane had barely finished filling him in when Grady rushed from the room. "I've got to find her."

Scarcely ten minutes later a commotion down the hall announced the arrival of more family.

They had all come, Stacey realized. As near as she could tell, every adult member of the Wilder family, and then some, crowded into the small waiting room.

Dane closed his eyes and held up his hands. "I don't want to know how you managed to get all the way from the ranch as fast as you did. I want no confessions."

"And you won't get any," Ace said. "My lips are sealed. Hi, Stacey. We saw Grady's truck outside. How's Rachel?"

"We haven't heard anything since they wheeled her away," Stacey answered.

Ace immediately started introducing her to everyone. She met his wife Belinda who, with her dark hair and lively, intelligent gray eyes, seemed like a good match for the rancher. Then there was Jack and his wife, Lisa, and their baby who was just under two years old.

Stacey was fascinated to learn that the baby's name was Jacqueline Dana. Jacqueline for her father, of course, but Dana was for the man who drove the car while the baby was born in the back on the trip into town. None other than Dane himself.

"My, Sheriff," Stacey teased. "You seem to have

a thing for women about to give birth. I guess that's what the nurse was talking about when we first got here. Maybe you're in the wrong line of work.''

Dane gave an exaggerated shudder. ''Perish the thought. All I did either time was drive.''

''Come on, Dane, don't be so modest.'' This came from the youngest brother, Trey. ''I remember you telling me about that woman in the back seat of your patrol car down in L.A.''

Nothing would do but that Dane tell the story. If he didn't, he was warned, he would be badgered to death until he gave in. So he told about being a rookie cop and having to help a woman give birth in his car.

Somehow, during the telling, Stacey met Laurie, Trey's wife, and their six-month-old daughter, Katy.

''Donna—that's Ace and Belinda's housekeeper,'' Laurie explained to Stacey, ''had some errands to run in town this morning, so she took all the kids to school. We left word for her to stop here on her way home and pick up Katy and Jackie. They'll get too fussy if Rachel's labor lasts very long.''

''Let's hope it doesn't,'' Dane said. ''Grady didn't look like he could handle it.''

*Oh, and you were doing so much better,* Stacey thought with a secret smile.

They all helped themselves to the coffee in the urn on a small table in the corner. Ace asked about Stacey's ankle.

''Much better today,'' she said, demonstrating her new, albeit cautious and slow, walking ability.

''I like your shoe combination,'' Belinda said. ''It makes a statement.''

''How did you hurt it?'' Lisa, Jack's wife, asked.

Stacey shot Dane a look. "I got blinded by a flash-light and lost my footing. Fell down a ravine."

"I take it from that look you just gave Dane," Trey said with a deep chuckle, "that it was his flash-light?"

"You guessed it," Stacey said.

"Smooth move, Dane. Is this some new way to pick up women?"

"Trey, shame." His wife gave him a dark look.

"Hey," Trey protested. "Don't look at me, it worked."

Dane smirked. "At least I didn't have to put an ad in the paper to meet a woman."

Laurie laughed uproariously while the rest of the family joined in. "He got you there, Trey," she told her husband.

Not long afterward a nurse came to tell them Rachel was settled in the birthing room, and that everyone was welcome to join her there for a while.

Stacey was surprised that a hospital this small even had a birthing room.

"I'll just wait here," she said.

"Me, too," Dane said.

"Oh, no." Lisa shook her head. "I know Rachel will want to see you, Dane. And we've got tons of questions for Stacey," she added with a grin. "You two come right along with the rest of us."

"She's right." Ace slapped Dane on the shoulder. "You get mixed up in one birth in this family, you can't get out of this new one. But don't everybody hound Stacey with questions," Ace warned the rest of the family. "If she wants to talk about anything, she'll let us know."

Stacey smiled in gratitude. She had planned to tell

them everything she knew once she got to their
house, but she had yet to decide just how to go about
the telling. She wasn't prepared. She needed a little
time to think things through.

It was a boisterous group that trooped the otherwise quiet halls of the hospital to the birthing room
at the far end of the building. They tried to be quiet,
continually shushing each other, but they were so
giddy with excitement over the imminent birth of the
next Wilder that they couldn't seem to contain themselves.

The birthing room was spacious, furnished and
decorated in cool colors, with whimsical baby animals painted on the walls. It was complete with a
bed and a special recliner for the mother-to-be, and
a sofa and three chairs making up a family seating
area.

Rachel occupied the recliner. Grady had drawn up
a footstool and sat next to her knees, his hands cra-
dling hers. It was the sweetest sight Stacey had ever
seen.

"There you are," Rachel cried when the family
trooped in. "I knew you wouldn't make us go
through this alone."

Within twenty minutes, Donna Harris, Ace and
Belinda's housekeeper, as well as Lisa's aunt,
showed up to collect the two youngest Wilders. No
sooner had she departed than Alma Helms, the Lewis
housekeeper who had raised Grady since his mother
died when he was a boy, and her husband Joe, who
managed the Lewis ranch with Grady, arrived. They
weren't about to miss the birth of Grady's child.

The next four hours were an education for Stacey.
She'd never been so intimately exposed to such a

large, warm and loving family as this one. She was the only child of an only child, and she'd grown up in a house filled with more tension and angry words between her parents than love.

It was also an education watching Dane interact with these people who did not know he was their brother. When he thought no one was looking, she could see the yearning to be a real part of them in his eyes, an acknowledged member of the clan rather than the outsider he felt himself to be.

Yet they didn't treat him as an outsider, but as one of their own, and went out of their way to treat Stacey the same.

"You should have seen the double take I did," Laurie was telling her, "the first time I met Dane. That was last summer before Trey and I were married."

Stacey nearly did a double take of her own. Laurie and Trey were married last summer, and they had a six-month-old daughter? Ah, well, these things happened, and it was certainly none of Stacey's business.

"We were having a Sunday cookout," Laurie went on, "so the whole family was there. It was the first time I'd met them all. There we were, my girls and I, with our pale skin and blond hair, surrounded by all these black-haired, blue-eyed gods."

This got a round of hoots from the men.

"And goddesses," Laurie added, for Rachel and the three wives all had dark hair, too. "I was feeling like some kind of pale alien."

Stacey looked around the room, cognizant of her own blond hair. "I see what you mean."

"Then here comes Dane," Laurie said, "looking

enough like the rest of them that I thought maybe he was a brother they'd forgotten to mention.''

Stacey could only be grateful that the sip of coffee she'd just taken had been a small one, or she might have choked.

"Are you all right?" Lisa asked.

Stacey coughed again to clear her throat. She glanced over at Dane and found him with his back to the room as he looked out the window overlooking the empty field next door.

"I must have swallowed wrong," she finally said.

Ace and his brothers shared a quick, odd look, then peered around at Dane.

"We get that now and then," Ace said mildly. "I never saw the resemblance, myself. Did you, Jack?"

Jack eyed his older brother carefully. His only answer was a shake of his head.

Trey shrugged. "Why don't we just adopt him? He's practically one of the family anyway."

"There you go," Laurie said. "Problem solved. What do you think, Dane? Want to be adopted into this wild bunch?"

Trey grinned. "Don't you mean Wilder bunch?"

"Oh, groan." Laurie rolled her eyes.

At the window, Dane's ears turned an interesting shade of red. Stacey winced. She could only imagine what he must have been feeling just then. Why didn't he just tell them the truth? This was the perfect opportunity. But he stood at the window, his back stubbornly turned.

"Come on, now," Belinda said. "You're embarrassing poor Dane." She crossed to his side and patted him on the shoulder. "Don't pay any attention to these idiots, Sheriff."

Finally he turned toward the room. There was a good-natured smirk on his face. "Don't worry, Belinda, I never take them too seriously. But speaking of serious, Stacey's got some information I think you'll all want to hear."

She was going to kill him. There wasn't a doubt in her mind. She sent that message to him as clearly as she could with a sharp look. "It'll keep. This is a family time."

"Come on, Stacey," Rachel said as a contraction eased its grip on her. "Is it about the stranger in the grave? You know who he is, don't you? Tell us. Please?"

Stacey shot Dane another look that said, *I'll get you for this.* She wasn't ready. She hadn't decided on the right words. And now, thanks to him, she was out of time. Eight members of the Wilder family—nine counting Dane—looked at her expectantly.

Stacey was saved by the labor nurse, who came in and ran everyone out except Grady so she could check Rachel's progress.

As one they all went back to the waiting room. If Stacey had thought she was off the hook, she was wrong.

"So who is he, Stacey?" Ace asked. "The man in our cemetery."

Everyone looked at her expectantly.

She fought a sigh of resignation. "My grandfather."

"Here, sit down." Lisa seemed to be a born caretaker. "Have some coffee and tell us what you can."

She was reluctant to begin. They'd been so warm to her, open and friendly, including her in their conversations. She'd never been exposed to a family such as this and she was loath to do anything to upset them. To make them shut her out. How were they going to take what she had to tell them?

After two sips of coffee, she could no longer put it off, so she began. She told them everything she'd told Dane, about her grandfather ranting and raving that the Wilders had stolen from his family. How he took off one day before she was born and no one ever saw him again. How she didn't know why her grandmother hadn't come forward to identify him when his likeness was broadcast on all the television stations in the state.

"They were pretty poor," she said. "It was before I was born. For all I know they didn't have a television."

"When he didn't come home," Ace said, "wouldn't she have reported him missing? From there the police should have been able to make the connection. Right, Dane?"

Dane shrugged. "I would think so."

"It could be she was afraid to go to the police," Stacey said. "She never knew how he died, only that he was found dead on your ranch. Since he'd come here to make trouble, maybe Gran thought he'd found it. I know she never wanted anyone to know who that man in the grave is, but I don't know why, and I'm breaking my solemn oath to her by telling you this. But I think you have a right to know."

"And we appreciate it," Ace said. "I know it couldn't have been easy. But since the day Stoney found him out there in the snow, it's been eating at us that we didn't know who he was. We've always assumed he was just some poor drifter who got caught out in the cold and died. Now you tell us he came here on purpose because he thought we'd cheated his family out of something. Lord knows our father was a hard man, but I never knew of him to treat anyone unfairly.''

Trey snorted in disgust.

''Well,'' Ace said, ''anyone outside the family, at least.''

Trey snorted again.

''Okay, he never cheated on a business deal. He wasn't a cheater, except when it came to his marriage, and since it got us Jack, we can't, in all fairness, hold a grudge against him for that.''

One side of Jack's mouth curved up. ''You're all heart, bro.''

Stacey blinked. ''You're their half brother?'' she asked Jack. Then she pressed her fingers to her lips. ''I'm sorry. That's none of my business.''

''It's all right,'' Jack said easily. ''It's no secret. You must be the only person in the county who doesn't know. Yeah, I'm their half brother. But I don't think any the less of them for it.''

Ace let out a hoot of laughter that ended in a pained *oomph* when his wife's elbow connected with his ribs.

''What'd you do that for?'' he cried.

She leaned over and planted a smacking kiss on his mouth. ''Because you're such a dope, but I love you anyway.''

''I'm the dope? If you're gonna elbow somebody, go after Jack. He doesn't hold it against us,'' he added, mimicking Jack's smug tone.

Lisa jumped in to defend Jack, but Jack told her he didn't need defending. Then Trey complained that there was always a female around to defend Jack.

Even when he first came to live with them, Rachel, only five at the time, had defended him.

Before the teasing could get out of hand, Ace called a halt and turned to Stacey. "We kind of got off track. There's one thing you didn't tell us, Stacey. What was your grandfather's name?"

She glanced at Dane, and he gave her a nod of encouragement. "Ralph Conner."

There was a sharp, collective intake of breath.

After a long moment of silence, during which everyone stared at Stacey, Ace finally spoke. "Did you say Conner?"

"I'm sorry," Stacey said. "I guess I forgot to mention that what he said your family stole from his family was your ranch. The Flying Ace."

"My God," Ace breathed in wonder. "Then you're…" A big grin spit his face. "You're Jeremiah Conner's what, great-great granddaughter?"

She nodded once. Why was he smiling? Her family was accusing his family of cheating.

"Wait," Ace said. "Your middle name. What is it?"

"Conner."

"Hell, sweetheart." Ace opened his arms and swept her up in a big bear hug. "Welcome home."

Voices swirled in Stacey's head.

"Isn't this exciting?"

"How romantic."

"After all these years, a real live Conner at the Flying Ace again."

"Well, close, anyway."

"She was there the other night. That counts."

"Who would have thought."

"Rachel will love this."

"Hey! Now we can have that headstone engraved with her grandfather's name."

Amid all the excitement, Stacey caught a glimpse of Dane's face and nearly wept. Never had she seen such a look of longing on a man's face. This was *his* family, yet they didn't know it. Instead, they were acting as if she were one of them. They were taking her into their hearts and making her feel a welcome the likes of which she'd never known. And all Dane could do was look on and try to smile.

Since lunchtime had come and gone, Dane volunteered to make a run over to Main Street for sandwiches. Stacey went with him. No one seemed to question that she would.

"They've paired us," Stacey said, dumbfounded, once they stepped outside the hospital.

"What are you talking about?" Dane asked, his mind still back there with the Wilders joking about adopting him.

"The Wilders," Stacey said. "When you said you'd go get food, they automatically assumed I would go with you."

Dane paused in front of the Blazer. She had his attention now. "Paired us? Why would they do that?"

"Why would they accept me, more than accept me, the way they just did? Why would they make jokes about adopting you? They're crazy, that's all I can figure. But, oh, Dane." She placed a hand on his arm. "You should have told them. Right then when they were making those lame jokes about adopting you."

"No." He shook his head and moved to open the

passenger door for her. "This is Rachel's day. If I was ever going to tell them, it wouldn't be today."

"Then why," she said, her eyes narrowing, "did you throw me and my grandfather at them? That could have waited for another day. Should have waited. But, oh, no, you needed to divert their attention from you, so you used me."

Dane said nothing while he helped her up into the seat. Once he was behind the wheel and backing out of his parking place, he admitted she was right. "I'm sorry. I did use you."

He sounded so remorseful that Stacey ached for him. "It's all right." She reached out and touched him again, on the arm. Somehow touching him, connecting with him physically, helped steady this shaky feeling inside that had started the minute the entire family flooded into the quiet waiting room. "They're so overwhelming."

"I thought that might be what you were feeling when Ace hugged you."

She shook her head, trying to put her thoughts into words. "They each seem to know what the others are thinking. And the love…" She shook her head again. "I've never seen a family so filled with love for each other. And trust, and respect. They're… amazing. Oh, Dane, I wish you would have told them the truth. Will you ever?"

Last week, yesterday, he would have said an emphatic no. Now, after today… "I don't know. I don't know how I can after all this time."

She smoothed her hand up and down his arm. Such a simple touch, a gesture of friendship, nothing more, yet it eased the tightness deep down inside him. It almost scared him how glad he was that she was with him, that she'd been with him all day. He was sure that without her, he would have made his excuses and left the hospital hours ago. And he would have missed out on being around the people he cared most about in the world.

Yes, he was glad Stacey was with him. But it only made him want her more. How was he supposed to deal with this crazy attraction he felt for her, plus the emotions trying to surface from being with the Wilders all day, and catch a ring of cattle rustlers?

"You'll find a way," she said softly.

For a minute Dane worried that he'd voiced his concerns aloud. Then Stacey spoke again.

"They're your family. You need them, and they need you. I'd give anything for a big, boisterous, loving family like that."

Dane felt a bittersweet smile coming on. "Didn't you hear Ace? They've already decided you're one of them."

"Not the way you are. Or could be."

After Dane and Stacey returned and everyone devoured the beef and turkey sandwiches the café had fixed, they all ended up back in the birthing room for a while. But when Rachel's contractions started coming faster and harder and she started snarling at her brothers' lame jokes, the nurse finally cleared the room of everyone but Rachel and Grady. This time, they thought, for the duration.

But before the contractions had started coming so close and hard, before the snarling, Rachel had demanded to know everything Stacey had told the family about the stranger in the grave.

After the retelling, Rachel had wondered aloud

how Stacey had ever found the cemetery. "I mean, it's not like it's on any road map."

"Two sets of tracks."

All eyes turned to Jack.

"A couple of times in the past few years," he said, "I found the tracks of two people. Both with small enough feet to belong to women."

"My grandmother brought me," Stacey confessed. "She wanted to make sure I knew how to find the grave."

"But how did *she* ever find it?" Rachel asked.

"Come on, honey," Grady said to his laboring wife. He glanced down at their joined hands with a pained expression. She was clearly about to break his fingers with her fierce grip. "You need to relax."

"I am relaxed." She practically growled the words. "Come on, Stacey, tell. Take my mind off the coming blessed event. And I'd like to get my hands on the idiot that coined that phrase."

"It was a man," Laurie said. "You can bet on it."

Ace grinned. "I think the saying refers to the arrival of a new life, not the labor a woman has to go through to produce it."

Rachel, Belinda, Laurie and Lisa, spoke at once. "Oh, shut up."

"Come on, Stacey, how did you grandmother find our little family cemetery?"

Stacey shook her head. "I don't know. When I asked, she just said she had her ways."

In the grip of a new contraction, Rachel huffed out one quick breath after another and squeezed Grady's hand hard enough to make him wince.

"Get over it, pal," Belinda told him. "It's nothing compared to what she's going through."

"I'm not complaining," Grady protested.

The nurse ran them out a short time later, promising that it was almost time.

"That's what she said an hour ago," Dane muttered as the group made its way back to the waiting room again.

While they waited, Ace asked Dane if there was any progress on finding the cattle rustlers.

Dane cast a brief glance at Stacey, then nodded. "There is, but I'm not at liberty to talk about it just yet."

Ace narrowed his eyes. "Has the sketch artist come, then?"

"No." Dane shook his head. "I've called him off."

"Off?" Ace cried. "What the hell'd you do that for?"

"Because," Dane said, "Stacey was able to identify two of the men she saw—the two she said she would recognize—from photographs."

"Well, that's more like it. Why didn't you say so? Who are they?"

Dane studied the man who had been his friend these past two years. The older brother he couldn't acknowledge. "If you knew who they were, what would you do?"

Ace shared a look with Jack and Trey. Apparently they had discussed the case and had reached some sort of decision, for they didn't need words. They merely nodded once toward each other.

Dane widened his stance and folded his arms across his chest. They might be his brothers, but he wasn't going to stand for any vigilantism, if that's what they were planning. "I think you better tell me what that just meant."

"It meant that we've talked about it and agreed that if you want our help, we're ready and willing to do whatever you tell us to do. If you don't, we'll stand back and let you do your job however you see fit. But if we know who did it, and if we happen to run across them—no, we won't go looking, you have our word on that, but if we happen onto them—we'll hold them for you."

Dane let out the breath he'd been holding. This was better than he'd feared. He'd been worried that they might take off on their own. Knowing who they were after, Dane feared somebody would get hurt. Wilson and James were not going to take kindly to being caught. Dane would just as soon the risks involved remain with him and his deputies, and not civilians.

"Fair enough," he told them. "I appreciate it."

"Hell, Dane," Ace said soberly, "we know you'll get them if anybody can."

"Oh, I can," he said darkly.

"You know who they are?"

"I do. I don't have a warrant yet, because all I've got is one eyewitness who saw them at dusk while she was trespassing on private property. I've put the word out on the rig they used to haul the cattle, but so far, nothing has popped."

"Stacey's not enough?"

Dane shook his head. "No, and they've already tried to shut her up, which is why I'm sending her out to your place."

"And she's more than welcome," Ace said, meaning it. "Are you going to tell us who it is?"

Dane studied Ace, then looked around the room at the rest of the family. He heaved out a sigh and braced his hands low on his hips. "Since there's every chance that you might run into one or both of them on a trip to town or something, I'll say this. If you come across two former county deputies, the two I had to fire when I took office, be real careful."

"Hell and damnation," Jack said. "Ed Wilson and Farley James?"

"Ordinarily your basic cattle rustler is only after a quick buck. But these two will be armed, and I consider them very dangerous. I don't want any of you getting hurt. If you see them, you let me know and I'll take care of it. Do I have your word on that?"

"If I see either one of those jackals, I'm not about to let them walk away," Ace said with a snarl.

"Dammit, Ace, you just said you'd let me handle it."

"I said we'd hold them for you. And believe me, it will be a real pleasure. Now we've got more reason than just that beating they gave Grady a couple of years ago."

"Damn right," Trey and Jack said together.

"That is not what I wanted to hear," Dane said grimly. "You have to let me handle it."

The three Wilder men shared another look, another nod, then Ace spoke again. "All right. You handle it. We won't go looking for them. But if they happen to cross our path in the normal course of business, we're not letting them walk away if we can help it."

Dane knew when to push and when to ease off.

Ace, Jack and Trey were not going to back down
from their stance, and neither was he. There was no
point in arguing about it. He seriously doubted that
they would run across Wilson and James before Dane
had enough evidence to arrest them. He hoped.

He gave them another nod. "You trust me to do
my job, and I'll trust you not to do anything that
might get yourselves hurt or arrested."


An hour later, David Raymond Lewis, named for
Grady's brother and father who'd both been killed in
a plane crash two years earlier, made his entrance
into the world.

Rather than expose the newborn to a roomful of
people, regardless of how eagerly they had awaited
his arrival, he was taken to the nursery. The family,
plus Dane and Stacey, gathered outside the big glass
window as Grady held his son up and showed him
off.

"Look at all that black hair," Belinda said.

"The poor kid didn't stand a chance for anything
else," blond-headed Laurie joked. "Not with a
Shoshone for a father and a Wilder for a mother."

Dane stared through the glass at the tiny baby, all
red and wrinkly in Grady's hands, and felt a tight-
ening in his chest. Was this as close as he would get
to a family of his own? A child of his own? The
thought had never bothered him before, that he might
never marry and have children. So why, here and
now, was his gaze drawn from the baby to the
woman at his side? And why did this terrible sense
of yearning that he'd lived with since getting to know

the Wilders seem to change focus in that moment? Now it had nothing to do with Ace, Jack, Trey or Rachel. Now it had to do with a blue-eyed, angelic trespasser with an alias.

## Chapter Eleven

It was after dark when the group finally broke up and left the hospital. They seemed reluctant, Stacey thought, to leave the baby and Rachel, even though both were sleeping the sleep of the exhausted.

"Do you have a bag in Dane's car?" Ace asked Stacey.

"What?" His question took her by surprise. Only after she asked what he meant did she remember that Dane had been taking her to Ace's home that morning when they'd come upon Rachel.

She couldn't go home with the Wilders now. Not tonight, after this day of family closeness. It was bad enough that she had intruded, no matter what they'd said about her welcome.

"A bag," Ace said, a teasing glint in eyes that were almost the exact same shade as Dane's. "Clothes? Makeup? Stuff?"

"Oh, uh, well, yes. In Dane's unit." She couldn't do this. Couldn't leave Dane to go home alone, couldn't bring herself to leave him. Not yet. Another day, that's all she needed. A day for the Wilders to settle back into their routine after the birth of their newest family member.

A day to put a little distance between her and all the emotions that family stirred in her. She very much feared she had come to care for them entirely too much. She needed time to steady herself. Away from them.

"We'll get it, then, and you can ride back with us, save Dane a trip."

Beside Stacey, Dane bit back a protest. They would think he was crazy if he protested. He wanted her to go home with Ace, where she would be safe while he tracked down his former deputies. But somehow, during the day, he'd forgotten that he would be going home alone, that she wouldn't be with him. He was so used to her company, so used to thinking about her, being around her, it was going to seem odd without her. Lonely.

"But I can't go," Stacey said, her words rushed one on top of the other.

Dane stared at her, wondering what she was up to. He tried to decipher the look she gave him, but wasn't sure what it meant. Her eyes seemed to be pleading with him.

"What do you mean, you can't go?" Ace asked. "I thought it was all settled?"

"You know we want you to come," his wife Belinda said.

"I know," Stacey said, her voice sounding almost desperate. "And it was all settled, but...but John,

Dane's detective, we saw him when we went for sandwiches.''

Dane frowned. They hadn't seen John. The tips of her ears were turning red. What was she up to?

Stacey flicked her tongue across her lips in a nervous gesture and darted another look toward Dane, then back to Ace. ''John said he had some more questions for me and asked me to come in to the office in the morning. Didn't he, Dane? I guess we just forgot to mention it when we came back, what with all the excitement about the baby.''

Dane's choices were few. He could call her a liar, but then, he couldn't, really. He could back her up, but tell her John had changed his mind and wouldn't need her after all. Or, he could play along and have her with him one more night. Maybe even kiss her one more time before she was out of his life for good. Which was exactly where she would be as soon as he arrested Wilson and James.

The decision, it seemed, was simple. ''That's right,'' he said. ''I guess I forgot to mention it. Like she said, the excitement and all. My apologies, Ace. I'm going to need her one more night. I'll call you tomorrow and give you an update.''

Ace Wilder was nobody's fool. He knew there was something odd going on, but he chose to keep that knowledge to himself and hope Dane knew what he was doing. ''Fair enough,'' he said. ''Whenever you want to bring her out to the house, you don't even need to call. Just bring her.''

''Thanks,'' Dane said.

''Yes,'' Stacey said, her voice sounding weak and thready. ''Thank you. I'm sorry for the inconvenience.''

\* \* \*

"What," Dane said, his voice tight with tension, "was that all about?"

It was so cold, even inside the Blazer, that his breath made white puffs in the air. He'd waited to voice his question until they were two blocks away from the hospital.

Stacey let out the breath she'd been holding. "I'm sorry. I just couldn't go home with them, not tonight. Not after a day like today."

"Meaning?"

"It was a day for closeness, for family. Tonight they'll want to talk about it, about Rachel's labor, about the baby. I have no business intruding on that. I just couldn't do it."

"You wouldn't have been intruding. Hell, we were both there all day. You saw how they treated us, as if we belonged. They wouldn't have considered your presence an intrusion. When Ace said 'Welcome home,' he meant it."

"He would welcome you, too," she said. "They all would."

Dane felt the ache around his heart, the ache he felt whenever he thought of the family he refused to claim. As he turned onto his street, he had to admit that Stacey was probably right. They would accept him. Once the yelling was done. They would not take kindly to realizing he'd waited two years to come clean with them.

"You know they would," Stacey added.

"Maybe." He backed into his driveway and killed the lights and engine. "But not tonight."

As was his habit, Dane had left a lamp burning in the living room. He had it on a timer so that if he didn't make it home, it came on at dusk and went off at midnight, to give the impression that someone was home. The precaution was probably not necessary in Hope Springs—they had very little crime. But old habits from the big city had stuck with him.

He helped Stacey off with her coat, then hung it with his on the coat tree beside the door. "Are you hungry?"

"No." She looked up at him, then quickly away. The light from the lamp made her hair glow golden.

"What's wrong?" he asked.

She used her crutches to move a few feet away from him. "Nothing."

"You're not using your foot. Did you overdo it? Is it hurting?"

"No. Just a little ache, that's all."

"Then why won't you look at me?"

She turned, then, slowly, until she faced him. There was an earnest plea in her eyes he hadn't seen before. "You will tell them, won't you? Soon?"

"Why is it so important to you?" Without thinking, Dane reached out with one fingertip and nudged a strand of hair off her cheek.

It was the barest of touches, almost not there at all, but it was enough to reignite that spark of awareness inside Stacey that had been banked since they had kissed last night in his office. "Don't." She turned her head aside, away from his touch.

Dane didn't need to ask what she meant. He'd felt it, too, that sudden, heated awareness. On some level he'd been feeling it all day. Feeling that, and much more. So much more that it was all jumbled up inside him and he didn't know what to do about it. She was probably right. He shouldn't touch her at all, not even casually.

But he wanted to. Wanted to badly.

"Why?" He wasn't sure if he was asking the question of himself—why did he want her?—or of her—why shouldn't he touch her?

She ducked her head and moved away. "You're the one who said it wasn't smart."

"I was talking about kissing you."

Slowly she turned back toward him and met his gaze with a directness that held him glued to the spot. "Yes," she said softly. "You were."

"What are you saying? That touching you is the same as kissing you?"

She sighed and sagged on her crutches. "I don't know what I'm saying. Don't pay any attention to me. After today I'm feeling a little shaky."

"You've been on that foot too long," he said, frowning. "Sit down and prop it up."

Stacey let out a chuckle and rolled her eyes. Wasn't that just like a man, to misinterpret every little thing? "I didn't mean that kind of shaky. I meant emotionally."

"And for that, you don't want me to touch you? You didn't seem to mind touching me last night in my office."

"No," she answered honestly. "No, I didn't mind. But you were right, it wasn't smart."

"Because you distract me."

Stacey didn't know what made her say what she said next. Maybe it came out because it was so huge inside her. Or maybe some part of her wanted to chance that he might feel the same. "Because it makes me want more."

In the wake of her confession, every argument about why they shouldn't get involved flew right out of Dane's head. "You can't tell me something like that and expect me to walk away."

"I'm just trying to be honest."

"Okay," he said, moving in on her. "That's fair. How's this for honest?" He took her face in his hands and kissed her.

This time there was no teasing brush of lip across lip, no soft, slow savoring. This time he showed her exactly what he was feeling. He dived in and devoured.

There was no time, no chance for Stacey to protest. No thought of protest. She wanted this. Wanted him. It no longer mattered that he was all wrong for her, that she was only with him temporarily. It only mattered that he want her, and that he satisfy the terrible yearning that threatened to suck her under until she simply disappeared. That would be all right, if only she could be sucked under and disappear with Dane.

It wasn't lost on her that she'd never felt this way about a man before, not even the one she had married. In a saner moment, these overwhelming emotions, this heated yearning, might terrify her. But now, this minute, they only made her return the kiss.

His mouth was hard and insistent, his tongue like hot, rough velvet. When his hands left her face she felt bereft. When he reached down and tossed aside her crutches, she felt grateful, for now she could wrap her arms around him and hold on tight.

He made her heart pound, took her breath away, and it was liberating in a way she'd never dreamed was possible. Then he pulled his mouth from hers and she gasped for air, certain she would wither and die on the spot if he didn't bring his lips back to hers. His name came from her on a gasp.

The sound of it, all breathy and desperate, nearly buckled Dane's knees. His chest heaved with the effort to draw in much-needed air. "If this is any indication," he managed between breaths, "I'd say we're both more than a little needy."

"Well," she said, her breath finally returning. "As long as it's mutual."

He nuzzled his nose into her hair. He loved the smell of her hair. "I've left you standing on one foot."

"Yes." She leaned into him, pressing her chest against his and making him want to groan, it felt so damn good. "You have."

He trailed kisses from her temple to the corner of her mouth. "Is that a problem?"

She turned her face until her lips brushed his. "It could be." Her tongue, that clever, clever tongue, crept out and took a delicate swipe at his lower lip. "Maybe you should take me somewhere so I can get off it."

Dane paused, pulled back enough to see her face. "Somewhere?"

"The couch?" With her hands behind his head, she pulled him down to meet her. "The bed."

Heat, white and hot, rushed to his loins. He couldn't remember ever being with a woman so bold about expressing what she wanted. He liked it. Liked it a lot. "The bed." Eagerly he swept her up in his arms and kissed her hard and fast. "Definitely the bed."

Not her bed, he decided swiftly. His. He wanted

her in his bed. When he laid her gently on the
comforter and joined her there he knew it was right.
She might be his only for a short time, but she was
his. He felt it in his bones. He'd been drawn to her
on a dark, lonely night, found her in the least likely
place he could find a woman. He'd claimed her with
the beam of his flashlight, and she'd been his. He'd
lifted her from the dirt and gravel of the ravine and
carried her to his car, and she'd been his. He'd fed
her, given her a place to stay, tended her injury.

Oh, yes, the lady was his. He went about claiming
her in the oldest way possible. But he wouldn't simply slake his lust, because there was more going on
between them than that. How much more, and how
important it might be, he didn't know. He only knew
that she was here, and she was willing, even eager,
if the way she threaded her fingers through his hair
and pulled him down for another kiss was any indication.

Her fingers in his hair sent shivers of excitement
racing down his spine.

He thought to take his time with her, draw it out
and make it last. Savor every sweet inch, every second, and rein in the driving impulse to take her here
and now. But her hands slid down his neck and over
his shoulders and started releasing the buttons on the
front of his shirt, and the next thing he knew they
were both naked and he was cradled, gratefully, between her thighs.

Then they were touching each other, everywhere.
Long, slow glides of flesh against flesh. Fast, eager
grasps, hand to hand, mouth to mouth, body to body.

Stacey had never felt such fire, such need. She'd
thought she'd known what she wanted in a man.

Nice. Tame. Someone who didn't get in her way, who let her call the shots.

But Dane was none of those things, nor did he seem to be the domineering type. For the first time in her life, she had found her equal. It was the headiest thing she'd ever known.

He cupped her breast in his warm, callused palm, flicked the tip with his thumb. She gasped, arching into the touch, silently begging for more. And he gave it, with his tongue and teeth and lips, tugging on some invisible wire that ran from her nipple to her womb, drawing open a yawning emptiness that only he could fill.

In the dim glow from the streetlight outside at the curb, the two bodies twisted and arched across the bed, taking and giving, his mouth at her breast, her hand reaching for his erection.

When she touched him, took him in her hand, Dane shuddered. No tentative touch, no shyness in her grasp. Simply a bold, confident woman pleasing him, demanding that he please her. He was helpless to do anything but oblige.

At the last minute he remembered the two condoms in his wallet and reached over the side of the bed for his jeans.

He didn't carry the packets because he had an active sex life. If wishes were horses...hell, they were so old, their integrity should probably be suspect. No, he carried them to show the local teenagers that every responsible person who ever hoped to have sex carried protection. Only irresponsible fools did without.

He pulled one packet from the wallet, tore it open

and put on the condom. His hands fumbled, he was so eager to sink himself into her.

Sink, hell, he wanted to thrust, hot and fast and hard, again and again and again until he felt her world explode and his along with it.

And then it was happening. She helped him finish unrolling the condom and nearly did him in in the process. Then she guided him home, and he inched into her, holding back, holding back, until she cried out and surged beneath him, taking him inside her hot, slick flesh, so deep he thought—prayed—he might never find his way out again.

He was so close to losing control that he held there, deep inside her, not moving. Concentrating on not hammering into her as hard as he could until they both begged for mercy.

But again she moved beneath him.

"Wait," he managed, his chest heaving with the effort of holding back. "Don't move or I'll explode."

She pulled her knees up to hug his thighs. "I want you to explode." Gently, slowly, she flexed her hips. "I want us both to explode."

With a low groan, he gave in to her body's demand and began to move. The friction was so damn good he wanted it to go on and on and on. Again and again, he thrust into her, withdrew, thrust again.

Stacey felt tears sting her eyes. Nothing in her life had prepared her for intimacy with this man. Nothing, not marriage, not sharing herself with another man, had ever fulfilled her the way Dane did, even though she had yet to reach that sought-for peak with him. Just having him inside her, feeling his powerful body quiver with need, knowing that for now, for this moment, they were one, made her want to both weep and shout with joy.

He took her higher than she'd ever flown, and when she couldn't stand the teasing torment another moment, he groaned and gave one final, earth-shattering thrust that destroyed everything she'd ever thought she'd known about pleasure.

Dane's breathing was the first to slow. That could have been because Stacey had a hundred and eighty pounds of man on top of her, but she certainly wasn't complaining. Not when it was this man, who had taken her to places she'd never known before.

"Are we alive?" she managed.

Dane raised his head from where he had buried his face in her hair. "Come again?"

Considering their present circumstances, his usual version of "What?" surprised a bark of laughter from her. "So soon?" she asked.

When Dane realized what he'd said, and how she'd taken it, he snickered. A moment later, still smiling, he looked down at her. With his hands bracketing her face, he stared, bemused by this woman he barely knew but whom he felt as if he'd known forever.

Had he ever laughed while in bed with a woman? If he had, he couldn't remember it. What power did this one have over him that she filled his every thought and made him do things he knew he shouldn't?

Stacey watched the smile fade from his face. "Don't," she whispered.

"Don't what?"

With the tip of one finger, she traced a line across

his forehead then down the side of his face. "Don't think."

"You're right. This isn't a night for thinking." He turned his head and captured her finger between his lips, licking it with his tongue.

The gesture sent shivers of awareness down Stacey's arm. "Oh, my."

"Dare I say it—come again?"

"Yes." Her smile was quick and wide. "You lick my finger like that again, and I just might."

Dane shuddered. "Be my guest."

"I'd rather have you with me when I do," she whispered.

With a slow smile, he reached over the edge of the bed for his wallet. He pulled out the remaining condom. "This is my last one."

"Then we better make the most of it," she told him. "Allow me." With a hand to his chest, she pushed him over and down onto his back. After taking the packet from him, she tore it open and slowly, slowly, rolled it into place. So slowly that Dane groaned.

"You don't like that?" she asked him.

"If I liked it any better," he said with a low growl in his voice, "I'd be finished."

They both laughed, but only until Stacey straddled his hips, then leaned down and kissed him.

They took their time. Time to savor, to taste, to discover what made the other's breath catch. Time to linger when those special places were found.

The fire between them built slowly, but burned even hotter than before. And soon the slow pace was not enough. She raised above him and, with his hands on her hips, settled over him.

Her breath left her on a moan. To have him fill her this way, to have a part of him become a part of her, was the sweetest of tortures.

Then Dane turned the tables and rolled with her until his weight pressed her into the mattress and her thighs cradled his hips. They strained together, hips pumping, hearts racing, racing, racing. Each thrust was harder, faster, than the one before. Each small peak of pleasure higher and higher until an explosion of body and senses ripped through them, and bound them together more tightly than either thought possible.

And afterward, they drifted off to sleep in each other's arms.

The phone rang at four in the morning.

Dane woke the way he always did, immediately and fully. He shifted Stacey's precious weight from where she slept draped across his chest. He hated to move her. It felt so damn good and right to hold her there.

But the phone didn't ring at four in the morning with good news.

He couldn't believe she was sleeping through the ringing, through his moving her. Then again, he thought with a secret smile as he sat up and reached for the phone, they had pretty much worn each other out before falling asleep.

The call was from his dispatcher. The Colorado state police had just located not only the rig Stacey had described, but also approximately two hundred head of cattle, fifty of which bore the brand of the Flying Ace.

"I'm en route to the office."

## Chapter Twelve

The sky was barely turning gray when Dane left the two-lane blacktop and turned the Blazer onto the gravel road that led to the Flying Ace.

He was worried. Stacey had barely said two words to him since he woke her up and told her he had to go to work. She hadn't complained. Well, except for having to wake up at all. She was definitely not a morning person, he thought with a slight smile. When he'd given her shoulder a gentle shake to wake her, she had grumbled and groused and snuggled deeper into the covers.

He should have kissed her awake. Would have, if time hadn't been pressing.

He did manage to kiss her before they left the house, and it had been sweet. So damn sweet. And hot enough to have him wishing he could take her back to bed.

But again, she hadn't complained about his having to go to work. Neither had she complained when she realized he was taking her to stay with the Wilders. But since then she'd had next to nothing to say.

"This isn't the way I would have planned this morning," he told her now as gravel rattled against the undercarriage of the Blazer.

Out of the ache in the region of her heart, Stacey managed to summon up a smile for him. "It's your job, Dane. I understand."

What brought on the layer of sadness that weighed upon her was the other thing she understood. He was close now to catching the rustlers. Her ankle was much better. Soon there would be no reasons left for her to stay in Wyatt County. Their time together might already be over, if this trip of his to Colorado went the way he hoped it would.

One night. That's all they'd had together. She'd known better than to get involved with him, but she hadn't guessed, would never have guessed in a million years, that her heart had just been waiting for the right time to take the big tumble. When he'd awakened her and told her they had to go, she'd known.

*Too soon!* her heart had cried. She'd wanted more time with him. More nights of sweet, hot loving. More days of work and conversation and laughter. More shared meals, more quiet drives. More arguments. That's when she knew. She was in love with him. Deeply, irrevocably, heartbreakingly in love. And for all she knew, she might never see him again after this morning. He could wrap up the case and have Ace drive her to get her car.

He probably wouldn't do that, though, she

thought. He was much too nice a man, too honorable to simply disappear without a word to a woman he'd just spent the night with. A woman he'd kissed at the front door of his house less than a hour ago as if there were no tomorrow.

"I don't know how long I'll be gone," he said.

"I know, Dane. It's all right."

"But I should be back sometime tomorrow at the latest. Tonight if things go well."

Beneath an arched sign that proclaimed they were entering the Flying Ace ranch, they crossed over a cattle guard.

He drove with his right arm extended, hand braced against the steering wheel. "Will you be here when I get back?"

The question startled her. He thought she wouldn't wait for him? That she would, what, have Ace take her to her car and go home to Cheyenne?

And why shouldn't he think that? She'd made it more than clear from the minute she met him that all she wanted to do was go home. When he left her at the ranch, it would be the first time they'd been separated for more than a few minutes, except for the afternoon she'd spent at the motel.

"I'll be here," she told him.

At her answer, Dane eased his grip on the steering wheel. She couldn't know, because he hadn't told her, how important it was to him that she be here when he got back. He couldn't tell her, not in words, because he wasn't sure he understood it himself. He only knew that if she left, she would take a big chunk of him with her. A chunk he wasn't sure he could survive without.

*Whoa.* How had this happened? How had this

angel-haired trespasser with an alias come to mean so much to him so fast?

All he knew was he thanked God for it, and for the arrangements to get her to safety before he let his guard down any further and got her hurt through his inattention to his job.

He would leave her with Ace and go to Colorado to interview the man they'd arrested for possession of stolen cattle. If the man could—and would—identify the men he'd gotten the cattle from, Dane would be able to get a warrant and arrest Wilson and James. With them under lock and key, Stacey would be safe. She would be even more safe for not being the only one who could place them with the stolen cattle.

Then...then he and Stacey would talk. Figure out what they were going to do. He couldn't simply let her walk out of his life.

He glanced at her, and their gazes met. There were feelings in those blue eyes of hers, feelings for him. They made his chest swell and his throat ache. He reached across the console and took her hand in his.

Stacey closed her eyes and entwined her fingers with Dane's. She held on tight and swallowed.

Neither spoke. They both looked straight ahead as the headquarters of the Flying Ace became visible in the distance. They looked straight ahead, and held on to each other.

Still a few minutes shy of sunrise, they pulled up next to a Flying Ace pickup at the rear of the main ranch house. Ace himself was standing on the back porch waiting for them, his hands tucked into the pockets of his shearling coat, cowboy hat pulled low over his eyes.

Dane gave Ace a wave, then turned to Stacey. "Ready?"

Ready, she thought. Ready to let go of his hand and watch him drive off? How silly of her, to let such a thing bother her. He was only going to do his job, not sail the seven seas for a couple of years.

Ready to let this big, warm family embrace her again? That was almost as scary as being separated from Dane. What did she know about families, except the dysfunctional kind?

But Dane didn't need her fears and insecurities. He needed a clear mind to concentrate on his job. So she dug deep and found a smile.

"Ready," she said.

He got her duffle out of the back, then helped her out of the Blazer and up to the house. The air had a serious bite to it this morning, courtesy of a stiff wind sweeping down out of the north.

Ace held the door open for them, then followed them into the mudroom, where they hung their coats and his hat on pegs on the wall.

Stacey welcomed the warmth of the house, even though she'd been exposed to the cold outdoors for less than a minute. She also welcomed the smells from the kitchen just beyond the mudroom. Neither she nor Dane had eaten yet. When he'd called Ace to tell him they were coming, Ace had told them to save their appetites.

"Your wife's not cooking, is she?" Dane had asked with a laugh.

Ace had apparently said no, his wife was not cooking. They would be safe.

There must surely be a joke in there somewhere,

but Stacey hadn't asked and Dane hadn't volunteered.

Donna, their housekeeper who had come to the hospital the day before and taken the two youngest Wilders home with her, turned from tending a skillet full of bacon and greeted them.

"You're here," she said. "Good. Breakfast will be ready in ten minutes."

Belinda, Ace's wife, came in and showed Stacey to the guest room. Dane followed, carrying Stacey's bag, then they rejoined Ace and Donna in the kitchen.

Over a huge breakfast of bacon, scrambled eggs and pancakes, Dane updated the others on what had happened in Colorado. He'd already told Ace that his missing cattle had been found, when he'd called the ranch earlier.

"But don't expect to get them back very soon," Dane warned now. "They're evidence. I'll do what I can to get the guys in Colorado to hurry things along."

"I appreciate it," Ace said.

After breakfast, when Dane was getting ready to leave, Donna presented him with a thermos of hot coffee.

"For the road," she told him.

"Thanks, Donna. And thanks for the breakfast. You get tired of working out here, I'll hire you to cook for me."

"Hey, go find your own cook," Ace protested.

"Ah," Belinda said with a grin. "Spoken like a man who doesn't want his wife in charge of meals."

"She knows me so well," Ace responded.

Stacey eyed the two Wilders, more than halfway

expecting a heated argument to break out. After all, the husband had just denigrated the wife's cooking. Even if Belinda couldn't cook, a comment like that, especially before outsiders, would have raised the roof in her house when she was growing up.

Belinda caught Stacey's wary look and laughed. "Don't worry," she said. "There are no fireworks in the making here. It's not that I can't cook, it's that I resent being expected to do it simply because I'm lower on testosterone than he is. To get even, if I have to cook I generally let the boys plan the menu."

"The boys?" Stacey asked.

"Our sons," Belinda said. "Ages five, seven and nine."

Stacey blinked. "Oh." Little boys planning the menu could be…interesting, she thought, fighting a laugh.

Ace gave an exaggerated shudder. "The last time, we had SpaghettiOs and Gummi Bears."

"Gummi Bears. For dinner?" Stacey asked carefully.

Ace shot his wife a narrow-eyed look. "Breakfast."

Belinda's grin sharpened. "They don't ask me to cook often."

Dane said his goodbyes and shook hands with Ace, then turned to go. Stacey followed on her crutches as he went to the mudroom. She watched, feeling a hollow emptiness in her middle as he put on his coat. She must have it bad, she thought, to feel so devastated at being separated from him for a day or two.

With his coat on, he came and stood before her. "I'll be back as soon as I can."

"Take care," she said. "Drive carefully."

He nodded. "I will." After a long look, he turned to go. He got as far as the back door before he stopped and turned around. "To hell with this." He crossed the three feet separating them in one stride, grabbed her by the shoulders and kissed her.

It was hard and hot and devastatingly thorough. When he released her and stepped back, all Stacey could do was stare.

Then he was gone and she was left staring out the storm door at his taillights getting smaller and smaller as he drove away.

When she finally turned back toward the kitchen, Ace, Belinda and Donna were standing side by side, watching her, with wide, matching grins.

Her cheeks burned like fire.

It was the longest day of Stacey's life, but also one of the most enjoyable.

Ace left the house for the barn a few minutes after Dane drove away. The kiss he planted on Belinda before he left was every bit as hot as the one Dane had given Stacey. Considering they'd been married for years, that said a lot to Stacey about the solidity of their marriage. And it reaffirmed her belief that she didn't have to settle for a repeat of the examples she had to go by—her own disastrous union and the unarmed conflict her parents had called marriage. It really could work. Ace and Belinda, and the rest of the Wilder family, were proof of that.

She tried to help with the kitchen cleanup, but with her ankle, she was less than agile, besides which, Belinda wouldn't hear of it.

"You're our guest," she said emphatically.

Stacey pursed her lips. "Yesterday your husband said I was one of the family."

"And he meant it," Belinda said. "That's how we think of you. Hell's bells, your great-great grandfather owned this land before any Wilder ever got here. That's got to be worth something."

"Yeah," Stacey said with a laugh. "It's worth one ace in a poker hand."

"All right. Here." Belinda tossed her a dish towel. "If you can stand on one foot you can dry the things that won't fit in the dishwasher."

No sooner had they finished cleaning the kitchen than three miniature copies of Ace Wilder raced into the kitchen, all talking at once. They were, Stacey soon learned, Jason, Clay and Grant, ages nine, seven and five, respectively, and they were a handful. An adorable handful, but no wonder the Wilders had hired a housekeeper.

Donna cooked another breakfast for the boys, then Belinda drove them to the bus stop out where the ranch road met the highway.

Lisa, Jack's wife, came over and brought little Jackie, and shortly afterward Laurie showed up with baby Katy in tow.

Stacey's friends at home were mostly young single women, and none of them were what she would consider close. Belinda, Lisa and Laurie were more than sisters-in-law, they were the closest of friends, and they included Donna with them, making no distinction because she was hired help. She was a friend as much as the others. The affection and respect among the four was a real eye-opener for Stacey. A longing for this type of friendship of her own began to grow inside her.

They tried their best to get her to talk about Dane, but she refused. She was afraid if she started talking about him, they would know the true depths of her feelings, and she wasn't ready to share them with anyone yet.

The five of them prepared a huge hot lunch, and when the men came in to eat, Stacey met a few of the ranch hands.

One of them, an old man who walked as if the horse was still between his legs, doffed his hat and bobbed his head. "You'd be the stranger's grand-daughter I've been hearing about."

He was Stoney Hamilton. "You're the one who found my grandfather."

He bobbed his head again and shuffled his feet. "Yes ma'am. It was a long time ago, but I just want you to know how sorry I am. If there'd been anything I coulda done to save him, I woulda done it, and that's for sure."

"I'm sure you would have," she told him, squeezing his hand. "I'm just glad someone found him. Thank you, Mr. Hamilton." She pressed a kiss to his cheek.

He turned so red and flustered that the other men whistled and laughed.

Throughout the meal, whenever anyone spoke of the stolen cattle and Dane's name was mentioned, they spoke of him with respect and confidence. It was plain that they admired his abilities as a sheriff, and that they liked him as a man.

Stacey wanted so badly to tell them that he was one of them. That they shared the same father. That he needed his family to be his family. But she'd given her word, so she kept silent.

After the meal, and the never-ending kitchen cleanup, the men went back out to work, and Lisa and Laurie took their babies home to tend to their own chores. Belinda, too, had work to do, on her computer in the office she'd made for herself upstairs. Stacey used the quiet time for a brief nap, to make up for the sleep she had so gladly missed the night before.

She told herself all day not to expect Dane to come for her that night. It was a long drive to Colorado and back, and he would need time to question the man they had in custody. No matter how badly she wanted him to return, she didn't want him driving while exhausted. He hadn't gotten any more sleep last night than she had.

So as the afternoon faded, and the boys came home, Ace called it a day and supper was served. There was no sign of Dane, no word from him, and Stacey told herself that was to be expected. He would come for her, but not today. Maybe tomorrow. Surely tomorrow.

She was limping around fairly well without her crutches after supper. Her ankle was finally healing. She would be able to drive by tomorrow.

Oh, God, she wished she hadn't thought of that. The idea of going home to her lonely apartment, once her most longed-for goal, was now the last thing she wanted. But Dane had never mentioned a future for them. Never mentioned that he was interested in seeing more of her after the case was solved.

Then again, she told herself, neither had she. Why was it his responsibility? She could let him know she was interested without expecting him to make the first move, couldn't she?

She wouldn't let herself speculate on how they could possibly maintain a long-distance relationship, if that was what they wanted. Would such a thing even work? How could it last? Then again, she thought, if her parents had lived several hundred miles apart, they might have had a much better marriage.

But she didn't know if Dane even wanted a relationship, long-distance or otherwise. The only way to find out would be to ask him. And if he didn't...if he didn't want anything more from her than what they'd already shared, she didn't know what she would do. Maybe murder him, she thought.

She would just have to do her best to make sure he wanted what she wanted. As soon as she figured out exactly what that was.

At eight o'clock, when Stacey was in the kitchen pouring herself another cup of coffee, headlights shot twin beams of light through the window over the sink as a vehicle turned to park near the back door.

Was it...? Could it be...?

She was afraid to hope. But who else would come way out here at this time of night?

Setting down her mug on the counter, she rushed to the back door, ignoring the twinge in her ankle, and peered out.

"Dane," she breathed. He had come.

He climbed out of his Blazer and started up the walk, his eyes locked on her. He looked tired, she thought. All those hours on the road, and whatever he'd had to do in Colorado concerning the case, on top of so little sleep. She supposed she should feel guilty for that, but she didn't.

She stood at the back door, her heart thundering.

Tired or not, he looked so incredibly good to her. She only wished she knew what he was thinking. Did he still want her, or had she been a one-night fancy for him?

No, she refused to believe that. And when he got closer, so that the porch light struck his face, she could see the intensity in his eyes and she knew.

"Dane," she whispered.

He came up the steps and nearly tore the door off its hinges before stepping into the mudroom and wrapping his arms around her. Without a word, he took her mouth with his and nearly swallowed her whole. She gave him everything his kiss demanded, and made a few demands of her own.

Had it been only a day since she'd last tasted him, felt his arms hard around her crushing her to his chest? It seemed as if it had been months. But he was here now, and kissing her as if he, too, had felt the same loss at their brief separation.

When he came up for air, they were both gasping.

"Isn't it sweet?"

Startled by Belinda's voice, Stacey whirled to find her and Ace grinning at them again from the kitchen doorway.

"Should I get a bucket of cold water to throw on them?" Ace asked.

Stacey blushed. Dane, obviously undaunted, hung up his coat then slipped an arm around her waist. "Not if you want to find out what happened today."

Ace called Jack and Trey on the phone and told them Dane was back with news, but Dane couldn't wait. He wasted neither time nor words in relating what had happened in Colorado. He was obliged to tell Ace what was going on, but he wanted to get Stacey to himself so badly that, for all he knew, he could be leaving out big chunks of information.

He knew he hit the high points, though. The man arrested in Colorado for possession of stolen cattle decided to spill his guts. He named names, gave dates, number of head stolen from which ranch. There were cattle from Utah, Idaho, Wyoming and Colorado, all on their way to a packing plant—once their brands were doctored—where an inspector was being paid to look the other way. The latter was for the feds to deal with.

But the Colorado man didn't hesitate to name Ed Wilson and Farley James as two of his suppliers. He volunteered their names, then picked them out of a photo lineup without a blink. Dane had his sworn statement, plus Stacey's, ready to back up a warrant for their arrest. If they showed their faces in Wyatt County again, they were his.

Ace was more than pleased with the news. He wanted Dane to wait around for Jack and Trey to get there so he could tell them, too, but Dane declined. As much pleasure as he took in the company of his three half brothers and their families, just then he wanted nothing more than to load Stacey into his Blazer and go home.

Which was exactly what he did, just as Jack and Trey arrived.

The three Wilder brothers stood in the doorway looking down the gravel road that led to the highway, much as Stacey had done that morning, at the disappearing taillights of Dane's Blazer.

Trey scratched his chin and held up a five-dollar bill. "I give them two miles."

"No way," Ace said. "You didn't see the way he greeted her."

"Liplocked her, did he?" Jack asked.

Ace chuckled. "Like a starving man at a feast."

"In that case, I say they won't make it more than one mile before he pulls over and does it again." Jack handed over his five.

"I'm in for a half mile," Ace said.

"If you win," Trey said, "it'll be because you had a firsthand look at them together."

"So did you, yesterday," Ace said.

"Yeah, but that was yesterday."

"Looks like Ace won," Jack said lazily as the taillights brightened with the addition of brake lights and the Blazer stopped at a point that the brothers knew was about a half mile from the house.

The five-dollar bills made their way happily into Ace's pocket. Ace looked out toward the tiny red lights a half mile away and smiled. "Good for you, Dane. You deserve a good woman, and I think you've found one."

"There's something I've been meaning to ask," Trey said.

"What's that?" Jack asked.

"What do you suppose that look on Dane's face meant when Laurie told that story about thinking he was another of our brothers?"

Ace draped an arm over each brother's shoulder. "You know, I've been wondering about that myself."

"Come on," Jack said. "We've all been wondering a little about him since he first showed up in town."

Trey frowned. "Even Rachel says when you put

him in a room with the rest of us, a stranger wouldn't be able to tell which one wasn't a Wilder.''

Jack eyed them both. "You know, don't you, that he was born in Cheyenne, two months after I was."

Ace narrowed his eyes. "Now why," he said with a shake of his head, "does that not surprise me."

"His mother was a waitress, same as mine. Except she worked in a restaurant instead of a bar."

"How do you know all this?" Trey demanded.

"I use my ears for something other than to keep my hat from sliding down over my eyes."

"Now, boys," Ace said with mock sternness.

Jack and Trey eyed their older brother with feigned malice. "You want first crack," Trey said, "or can I have it?"

From the doorway, Belinda propped her hands on her hips. "If there's any cracking going on around here, I'm the one who's going to do it. How far did they get before he stopped to jump her bones? It was hot enough around those two to melt concrete. Who won the bet?"

Ace beamed. "I did. A half mile."

## Chapter Thirteen

When Dane and Stacey drove away from the ranch headquarters down the gravel road that led back to the two-lane highway, neither spoke. The tension inside the Blazer was a living thing, taking up the space between them, the air around them. Dane drove as far as he could before slamming on the brakes and unfastening his seat belt as he reached for her.

"I'm sorry," he said harshly. "But I've been thinking about this all day." And he kissed her.

Stacey melted against him. "Me, too," she whispered between hot, fevered kisses as they practically devoured each other.

"It's crazy." He kissed her jaw.

"I know." She kissed his eyelid.

His lips trailed down her throat. "Missing someone so damn much in just one day."

She arched her neck to give him better access. "I know."

His mouth traveled back up to hers. Their lips meshed, their tongues mated, and his hand reached beneath her coat to cup her breast.

His name came from her lips on a sigh and a moan.

Dane knew he was losing his self-control. He forced a quick laugh. "Look at us. We're in an official county vehicle, and I'm about ready to rip your clothes off and have my wicked way with you."

"Wicked?" She ran her fingers through his hair. "Promise?"

He kissed her again, and what started out hard and hungry ended up soft and sweet. "Let's go home," he whispered against her lips.

"Yes." She nipped his bottom lip with her teeth. "Let's."

After one more kiss, then another, Dane finally turned to the steering wheel, buckled his seat belt and put the unit in gear.

They were another mile down the road when Dane's cell phone chirped. It was Ace, thanking him for stopping when he did to kiss Stacey, thereby winning Ace the bet.

"You jackass," Dane said with a laugh. "I'll get all of you for this."


They were ten miles north of the ranch cutoff on the highway when Dane spotted a van with its emergency flashers on parked at the side of the road ahead.

"Looks like somebody's having trouble," Dane said. He slowed and pulled over behind them.

Stacey's heart warmed. He wasn't even on duty, but he would stop. He was the type of person to help his fellow man whenever he could.

But she supposed his police and sheriff training was so ingrained that he automatically reached for his radio and called it in before he got out of the truck. "Sit tight," he said to her. "I shouldn't be long."

Another sign that his training was ingrained was that when he stepped outside, his coat unbuttoned, he automatically reached toward the small of his back to check his weapon. He probably did it unconsciously.

He was a good man. A genuinely good man. She was going to do everything in her power to hang on to him for as long as possible.

While she watched, he approached the driver's side of the van. From her position in the passenger's seat she had to lean left to be able to see him. As she did, her arm brushed the cell phone he'd tossed aside after getting the call from Ace.

Stacey grinned. They'd been taking bets, had they? She picked up the cell phone and pressed the recall button. Ace answered on the third ring.

"You made bets on us?" she said, laughter in her voice. "You should be ashamed."

"Not me," he protested.

"What do you mean, not you? You *won* the bet, from what I heard."

"I meant I shouldn't be ashamed," Ace said.

Stacey laughed. "Dane stopped to help someone in a van, so while he's out of the truck I just wanted to call and give you a hard time."

"Now who should be ashamed?" he said.

But Stacey was no longer listening. She had glanced up at Dane. He was backing away from the van with his hands in the air.

Ace was still talking in her ear, but she had no idea what he was saying.

Three men poured out of the van on the driver's side, all of them pointing guns at Dane.

"Ace," she cried into the phone. "Oh, my God, Ace, they've got guns."

"What? Who!"

"I don't know, I can't see their faces—no, wait, it's them! It's those two men who stole your cattle, I'm sure of it, and they're forcing Dane back to the truck at gunpoint. They're headed this way! What do I do?"

She should have used the radio and called Dane's office, Stacey thought, her mind running in terrified circles. But there was no time now, they would see her. They could probably see her using the phone. Oh, God!

At the other end of the cellular signal Ace Wilder was already on the move. He and his brothers had been in his office when Stacey called his cell phone. He snapped his fingers at Jack and Trey and pointed toward the gun cabinet.

"Stay calm, Stacey. You said there are three of them. Just do whatever they say, okay? Don't try anything. We're on our way. If you can let me know what's going on without them realizing you're on the phone, great. Otherwise, don't try it. Okay?"

"O-okay. Here they are."

Stacey's mouth was suddenly so dry she was surprised she could speak. Quickly she placed the cell phone beside her on the seat. Unless they looked closely or made her get out, no one would be able to see it. She hoped.

One of the men, the one she didn't recognize, turned away and ran back to the van. The other two held Dane beside the Blazer for a minute. They were talking, but she couldn't hear what they were saying over the sound of the truck's engine, which Dane had left running, and the blast of the heater. Then one of them got into the back seat, his handgun trained on Dane every second.

The second man ordered Dane to get in beside the first one. When Dane ducked to climb in, his eyes met hers. She read the look in them easily. He was furious, and he was afraid—for her. And he was trying to tell her everything would be all right.

When he was inside, the second man slammed the door and got into the driver's seat. He eyed Stacey up and down with a sickening grin.

"You're keepin' mighty pretty company these days, *Sheriff.*" He spat the word *sheriff* out as if it left a bad taste in his mouth. This one, Stacey thought, was Farley James. She remembered his name from Dane's office. He was the one Dane had stopped the other night for having no taillights.

"Of course," James went on, "she's got a big mouth on her, and I don't much like that."

"If she was the only witness against you," Dane said lazily, "I can't say I'd blame you. But Farley, I'll tell you, you need to pick a better class of men to do business with."

"What are you runnin' off at the mouth about?" the one in the back seat, Ed Wilson, demanded.

Dane chuckled.

How could he be so cool and relaxed, while Stacey

wanted to scream in terror? She had to slow her breathing. Act calm, like Dane. She couldn't panic. Couldn't curl up into a fetal ball and suck her thumb, which was what she most wanted to do at that moment, and stay that way until this nightmare was over.

"I'm talking about that fellow in Colorado," Dane said. "Hansen."

Wilson and James both snarled like a couple of pit bulls.

"What's that old cliché?" Dane asked. "Oh, yeah. He squealed like a stuck pig. Names, dates, number of head, the works. He kept real good records, too, all written down in a ledger."

"I told you we shouldn't have gone with him," Wilson growled from the back seat.

"Shut up." James put the truck in gear and made a U-turn, taking them back south, in the direction of the Flying Ace.

"Why are we turning around?" Stacey hoped her voice was loud enough to be picked up and transmitted by the cell phone at her side. "Town is back the other way."

In the seat next to her, James sneered. "We ain't going to town, little girl."

Stacey didn't know what to do but to keep talking, maybe distract them. She didn't like the way that Wilson man in the back kept aiming his gun at Dane.

"But we have to go back to town," she said, trying to sound both reasonable and a little flighty. "I have a dinner appointment."

"Whoo-ee, did you hear that, Ed?" James called over his shoulder. "She's got a *dinner appointment.*

Well, sister, you're just going to have to miss that
there dinner appointment."

Stacey heaved a big, dramatic sigh. "I suppose
you're right, if you won't take us to town. But that
nice judge is going to think I stood him up."

In the back seat Ed Wilson sputtered. "You were
gonna eat with Judge Martin?"

When he spoke, Stacey twisted around to look at
him. "Do you have to wave that thing around?" She
managed to sound both annoyed and worried.
"Somebody could get hurt."

"What, this?" He held the gun up and pointed it
at the roof. "That's what it's for is to hurt somebody."

Through the back window Stacey saw the van following them. "Look," she said loudly. "It's that van
you were in. Why is it following us? Where are you
taking us?"

James snarled. "You're just full of questions,
aren't you? If you'd minded your own business and
kept your mouth shut, you wouldn't be in this mess
now."

"Minded my own business?" she cried. "I *was*
minding my own business. It was you and your
friends who messed things up for me. Thanks to you,
I've been knocked down a ravine, ended up on
crutches, and stuck here in this Podunk little town
for days."

In the back seat, Dane's heart was about to pound
its way up his throat. He didn't know where she'd
gotten the idea, but Stacey was deliberately trying to
keep both men focused on her instead of him. And
she was doing a damn good job of it. If he wasn't

so afraid it would backfire on her, he'd be bursting with pride at her wit and ingenuity.

She was talking too loud, much louder than necessary. That was fear. She was scared, and he ached for her.

If anything happened to her, he hoped to God Wilson and James killed him in the process, because he wouldn't be able to live with himself. This was his fault. He'd had his mind on getting her home and crawling into bed with her. He'd gotten cocky. He hadn't paid attention. He'd let them get the drop on him as if he'd been a green rookie.

How he was going to get them out of this situation, he didn't know. But somehow he would. They were coming up on the turnoff to the Flying Ace. There was help there, if only he had a way of reaching them.

Dammit, he had a cell phone, but it was in the front seat. So was the radio.

"Look at all those pickups," Stacey said. Again her voice was loud.

But it got his attention. His and James's and Wilson's as they all looked ahead and saw four, no, five pickups pull out of the Flying Ace road one after the other.

In the front seat James started cussing.

"You're going to have to slow down," Stacey warned loudly, "or you'll run right into them."

"I'm gonna run right into you if you don't shut up." But he slowed, because he had no choice. And he swore, because he seemed to have no choice about that, either.

The Flying Ace pickups were stopping, pulling

sideways right across the highway two deep, block-ing both lanes.

"What the hell?" Wilson cried from the back seat. "Farley, what the hell's going on?"

"Damned if I know."

James was driving at a snail's pace now, because he was mere yards from the pickups, with nowhere to go. They had even blocked the shoulders so he couldn't go around.

James stopped, the Blazer's headlights showing the Flying Ace men, the brothers and their hands, armed with rifles, standing in the vee of their open doors.

James cursed again. He couldn't go forward unless he wanted to broadside the pickups. With them parked two deep, he had to know that would be use-less.

He couldn't throw the Blazer in reverse because the van they'd been in was right on their tail.

He bunched up his fist and pounded the steering wheel. "Damn those interfering Wilders!"

Dane didn't know what in the hell made Ace and the others pull out and block the road the way the did, and he didn't care. He might never get another chance. He made his move.

Wilson and James had taken the semiautomatic he wore at the back of his belt, but he'd never discussed in front of them the practice he'd learned in L.A. of wearing a backup piece in an ankle holster. He'd thought about doing away with it more than once since coming to Wyatt County, but he had never managed to break the habit. If this worked, he might just go back and kiss the instructor who'd insisted he get used to the extra weight on one ankle.

He glanced at Ed Wilson seated next to him. Wilson, as was James, was focused on the pickups in the road ahead. Wilson still held the gun in his hand, but it was aimed at the side window now rather than at Dane's head.

Dane leaned forward to look over James's shoulder. The movement had the added benefit of allowing him to reach his ankle. If only he could get the leg of his jeans tugged up far enough to allow him to reach into his boot without tipping Wilson off. At least it was the left leg he needed, the one away from Wilson. Of course, that meant he was going to have to draw it with his left hand, and he was not a left-handed shooter.

So be it. He would take what he could get and make the most of it. Stacey's life could depend on it.

"What's happening?" he asked.

James flipped the switch to turn on the red and blue flashing lights on top of the Blazer. Then he used the P.A. system to speak to the people in the road. "Get out of the way," he demanded. "Clear the road or I'll drive right through you, Wilder."

"Come ahead, then, you stinking rustler," Ace bellowed back, shouldering his rifle and taking aim.

Wilson and James both started swearing again.

Even from where Dane sat he could tell Ace had drawn a bead on Farley James. Leaned forward as he was, Dane could also see the sweat popping out on the back of James's neck.

He had his pant leg up. Now, if he could just…

"What do you want, Wilder?" James called over the system.

"You," Ace called back, "with your hands in the air."

"You better do something," Stacey said with a definite whine in her voice. "And fast. I have to go to the bathroom."

Her comment was so outrageous and unexpected that both bad guys gaped at her.

Dane reached his gun and pulled it from his boot.

Next to him, Wilson saw the move and cried, "Stop!" He lowered the barrel of his gun to aim at Dane. His finger tightened visibly on the trigger.

Dane knew that Wilson preferred a stiff trigger, as opposed to James's loose one, which was likely go off if you sneezed on it. If James had been beside him, Dane figured he would be dead by now. Instead, he had maybe half a second before he had a hole blown in his chest. He swung his right arm up and out and knocked James's arm up.

The gun went off, sending a bullet through the roof.

Stacey cried out.

James cursed. As he fumbled for the gun he'd laid in his lap and craned his neck to see what was going on in the back seat, Dane followed with his left hand and aimed his pistol at Wilson's head.

One down. But that left James.

From the corner of his eye Dane saw Stacey move. She reached around with her right arm toward Wilson and cried, "Freeze!"

James froze.

"Put your hands up," Stacey ordered harshly, "slowly. I'm real scared and my finger's sweating. I just might pull this trigger by accident."

Dane swallowed. *Trigger?* What trigger?

But James raised his hands. Dane had no idea why, since he knew Stacey didn't have a gun, but he wasn't about to question it. Neither could he hope James's compliance would last.

But suddenly men armed with rifles swarmed the Blazer. Doors were jerked open. Ed Wilson and Farley James were disarmed and dragged out. They offered no resistance as they were forced to lie facedown and spread-eagled on the cold pavement.

The instant Dane saw they were secure and couldn't cause any further trouble, he reached between the two front bucket seats for Stacey.

At his touch, Stacey threw herself halfway over the console to reach him. "Dane!"

"Are you all right?" His voice shook, and suddenly, now that the crisis was over, so did his hands.

"I'm okay. I think." She buried her face between his neck and shoulder and wrapped her arms around him as hard as she could.

Questions, a dozen or more of them blazed through Dane's mind, but they would have to wait. First he had to reassure himself that she was truly unharmed, that she was safe. The only way he knew to do that was to kiss her, so he did, over and over, all across her face and back to her mouth.

"God," he managed, his voice still unsteady. "I've never been so scared in my whole life."

"Me, neither."

"What just happened?" he asked, pulling back to look at her. Something niggled at the back of his mind. Some warning that there was something left undone. But he couldn't focus on it until he had an answer. "How did you get him to raise his hands? I know you didn't have a gun."

With a smile every bit as unsteady as Dane's hands, she held up the cell phone still clutched in her grip. "I jabbed him in the side with the hard rubber antenna."

Dane stared at the phone, then at Stacey, dumbfounded. "You used a cell phone to disarm an armed, known felon?"

"It was the only thing I could think of to do."

It was too much. The chance she'd taken was beyond outrageous. And it had worked. He threw his head back and laughed. "God, I love you."

"That's real sweet." A grinning Ace Wilder stuck his head through the open back door through which he'd recently hauled one of the former county deputies who had stolen his cattle. "But if you two are about finished, there's a little business out here to take care of."

Still holding on to Stacey, Dane grinned at Ace. "I don't know where you came from or what you're doing here, but I'm damn glad to see you."

"Same here, bro."

*Bro?* Dane blinked.

Ace ducked out of the door and turned away toward the other men surrounding the truck.

"Bro?" Dane looked back at Stacey. "You didn't…"

Her eyes wide, Stacey shook her head. "I didn't say a word, I swear. I wouldn't, Dane. Not when you asked me not to. Maybe it was just an expression."

"Yeah," Dane said. "That's probably it. Are you sure you're all right?"

"I will be once my heart stops pounding. And you?"

"I'm fine. But I've got some business out there to take care of. You stay in here where it's warm."

Then that something that had tickled the back of his mind, that told him there was more to worry about, burst through his brain. "The van." There was a third man, behind them in the damn van.

He whipped his head around to see out the back window, then slumped in relief. With red-and-blue lights flashing across the top of his unit, a Wyatt County deputy—good God, it was Donnie—had the third man facedown on the ground and cuffed.

With one sneaker and one fuzzy pink slipper, Stacey climbed gingerly from the Blazer, mildly surprised to realize her knees were actually going to hold her upright. She was grateful, because she simply had to get out and move around. She knew an adrenaline crash was coming, and then she probably wouldn't be able to do anything but collapse. Before that happened, she wanted to personally kiss Ace Wilder and every one of his brothers and hired hands right on the mouth, God love them every one.

She didn't know how much time had passed since Dane had drawn his gun and Ace and his men had taken the two creeps out and to the ground. Once Dane had left the Blazer she had sat there for some time watching him frisk and cuff the two. By the time she finally stepped outside another county unit had arrived. Between that one and Donnie, who had arrived in time to block the van from escaping, they had the three men safely in custody, two in the back seat of the second unit, one in Donnie's.

She watched as the two units turned around and

raced away toward town. Good riddance, she thought with overwhelming relief.

Most of the Flying Ace vehicles were also headed out. Only the three brothers remained talking to Dane as she approached.

"Hey," Trey called. "It's our cell phone heroine."

She smiled, but it wasn't easy. Mention of the cell phone reminded her of how terrified she'd been and made her heart race. "Could you hear anything?" she asked Ace.

"Enough," he said. "You did good, hon."

"Oh, Ace." She threw her arms around him. "Thank you for coming. Thank you." Then she repeated the process with Jack and Trey.

Ace cleared his throat. "I think we better unhand her before Dane hauls us in for stealing his woman."

Stacey stiffened and withdrew from Trey's hug. Sure, Dane had said he loved her a short time ago, but that, she was certain, had only been in reaction to everything that had just happened. They had survived. He was glad they were both alive. He hadn't really meant it.

"Damn right," Dane said. "It's called trespassing."

The Wilder men laughed.

Stacey blinked.

Ace pursed his lips, then nodded. "Yep, I was right. You're in love with her."

Stacey held her breath.

Dane looked at her, the glare from several sets of headlights casting harsh shadows across his face. "That's between Stacey and me," he said.

Her vision blurred and she had to look away. She

supposed that was as good as a denial. If he loved her, he would have said so, wouldn't he?

He did sidle up and put his arm around her, and that was some comfort, at least. Just then she was willing to take whatever he was willing to offer.

"I have a question for you," he said to Ace.

"Shoot."

She felt the tension in every line of Dane's body as he stared at the man before him.

"A while ago, when you stuck your head in the car."

"Yeah?"

Dane took a slow breath, then let it out. "What did you call me?"

Ace paused a minute, then said, "I guess you heard me plain enough or you wouldn't be asking. I'm right, aren't I?"

An icy blast of wind buffeted them, but Stacey seemed to be the only one who noticed. All eyes were on Dane.

"What makes you think I'm…"

Ace's eyes narrowed. "What's the matter? Can't you even say it?"

Jack stepped forward and placed a hand on Ace's shoulder. "What makes us think that you're another illegitimate son of a man who went through about a six-month period where he nailed everything in skirts, as long as she was several hundred miles from home? He had a real weakness for waitresses, you know."

Dane's swallow was audible.

"Hell." Trey shouldered his way past his brothers. "Enough of this tap dancing. Are you or are you not our brother?"

Another swallow, followed by a shudder hard enough to make Stacey, leaning against him, shake.

Then Dane gathered himself and raised his chin. "My father's name was King Wilder. I never met him."

Ace Wilder gave Dane Powell a wry grin. "Everything you've ever heard about him, both good and bad, is true. Welcome home, brother."

Stacey's vision blurred again. Then suddenly she and Dane were surrounded by laughing, back-slapping, bear-hugging Wilder men.

## Chapter Fourteen

It was four in the morning before Stacey and Dane made it to his house. They'd gone by his office first for Dane to take care of the paperwork on the county jail's newest residents.

Word had spread rapidly, and when they'd arrived, most of the county's deputies were there, outraged that two of their own—even if they were *former*— had stolen cattle and kidnapped the sheriff and Stacey. Dane had more volunteers for extra jail duty than he knew what to do with.

"Remind me," he muttered to no one in particular, "to thank those yo-yos for kidnapping us so I didn't have to go tracking them down. Saved us probably several days."

Stacey rolled her eyes. She was sufficiently recovered from their ordeal to feel more like her old self. "Oh, yeah," she said. "I'm *real* grateful."

She was, as far as Dane's deputies were concerned, the heroine of the hour for her trick with the
cell phone.

Later, when Dane and Stacey were finally able to
go home, they didn't even make it to the bed before
they had each other's clothes off. It had hit them both
at once when they'd entered the house just how close
they'd come to losing each other for good.

The living room was strewn with jeans and coats
and sweaters. And one lone fuzzy pink slipper. The
carpet was initiated in a way it had not been since
Dane had had it installed two years earlier.

They made love again, later, in the bed, and fell
asleep holding each other tight.

It was the sun streaming through the window that
woke them the next morning.

Dane woke first and lay still, staring at Stacey's
beautiful, peaceful face, storing up another memory.
Ace had been right. He was in love with her. But
what would she want with a man like him? He was
too old for her. He was a cop. She hated cops.

"You look so fierce," she said.

Dane started. He hadn't realized she'd opened her
eyes. "I was just thinking."

"Must not have been very pleasant thoughts."

They weren't, Dane silently acknowledged. They
were about as unpleasant as thoughts could be. So,
too, was what he had to say next. "You know, don't
you, that with Wilson and James locked up and your
ankle healing, you're free to go."

Her gaze darted away as she shifted to bunch the
pillow beneath her head. "Go?"

Was she already pulling away from him, emotionally if not physically? "Home," he told her.

She pulled the sheet up and tucked it beneath her arms. "Home."

Damn, he wished she'd look at him. "That's right. You're free to go home."

Stacey's heart started a pounding that she thought surely Dane could hear. He was offering her the thing she had wanted most only a few days ago. Now it was the last thing she wanted. With a deep breath, she raised her gaze to meet his. She was not willing to walk away. Not yet. Not without a fight.

"If I'm free to go," she said quietly, "then I guess that means I'm free to stay, too."

His fist bunched around a handful of sheet. In protest, she wondered, or hope?

"Stay?" His voice sounded rusty. "Why would you want to?"

Was he blind? Couldn't he see how she felt about him? "For you," she said.

Dane's breath backed up in his lungs and his heart decided to stop beating. "I'm ten years older than you are."

"So?"

"You don't like cops."

"There are one or two I've come to tolerate."

Dane swallowed. "One or two?"

A shrug of one gleaming, bare shoulder looked casual enough, but her fingers were twisting in the hem of the sheet. "Well," she said, "I like Donnie. He's cute and friendly."

Dane's heart started beating again with a hard, solid thud against his ribs. He nearly smiled, but was afraid to. He could still be reading her wrong. She might not want as much from him as he wanted from her. "Donnie?"

Stacey huffed out a breath and glared at him. Was the man being deliberately dense, or just perverse? He was going to make her come right out and say it. But, by damn, if she lay around and waited for him to get to it, their first child would be in college. "And you." She didn't mean to snap out the words, but fear and tension shortened her temper. She forced a slow breath.

"You want to stay, for me? You don't care that I'm a cop, one who's ten years older than you?"

The uncertainty in his voice, in his face, melted her heart and dissolved her temper. "I love you, Dane."

Dane's heart stopped again. "Stacey." His eyes slid shut in utter relief as he leaned forward and pressed his forehead to hers.

"And I think," she said, "that Ace was right and you love me, too."

"He was," he said, peppering kisses across her cheek and down her nose.

Before he could capture her lips, she said, "Good. Then I guess that means if I ask you to marry me, you'll say yes."

Dane snapped his head back and stared. "Are you asking me? To marry you?"

Stacey met that deep blue gaze and knew that no matter his answer, she would never love another man. "I am," she said. "Will you marry me, Dane?"

A slow, deep smile spread across his face. "I'd sort of thought to do the asking myself, but the answer is yes. I'll marry you. I love you, Stacey Conner Landers."

\* \* \*

At twelve noon that day, Stacey and Dane clasped hands and stepped into Harvey's Café on Main Street. The entire Wilder clan, except the children and Rachel, who was at home with the new baby, was waiting for them.

The next hour was filled with questions and plans for a big celebration—not only to welcome Dane to the family, but to welcome Stacey as well.

Dane sat through the entire two hours with a grin on his face and a lump in his throat. Never had a man been so blessed.

A few days later Stacey learned that her grandmother was finally home from Atlanta, so she and Dane drove to Cheyenne to tell her they were getting married.

When Gwen Conner learned about all that had happened and that Dane and Stacey were getting married, that the Wilders were not responsible for her husband's death, that they openly welcomed the Conners as part of their family and had already ordered the headstone to be engraved with Ralph's name, she broke down and cried.

"But Gran," Stacey said earnestly, "why the secrecy all these years? Why didn't you ever come forward and identify Grandad?"

Gwen sighed and wiped her eyes. "I suppose since you're marrying into the family—and a sheriff, to boot—I should get it all out in the open."

Stacey shared a look with Dane, then said, "Surely that would be best."

Gwen was quiet for a moment, gathering her thoughts. They were all seated around her kitchen table. To keep her hands busy, she got up and refilled their coffee cups, then seemed to come to a decision and nodded. "All right." She took her seat again and wrapped her hands around her mug. "A couple of days after Ralph left to go confront the Wilders, he sent me a big, heavy box. I couldn't imagine what was in it, so I opened it."

"Well?" Stacey demanded when her grandmother paused. "What was in it?"

"Twenty thousand dollars in cash."

Dane nearly choked on a sip of coffee.

"What?" Stacey cried.

"Before I could decide what to do with it, they were plastering his picture all over the television and in the newspapers saying he'd been found dead on the Flying Ace. I could only assume, since he'd never had more than two dimes to rub together, that he'd stolen the money. Maybe from the Wilders themselves for all I knew. I would have returned it, but I never heard any mention of that much cash having been stolen. Ralph wasn't much, but he'd been my husband for nearly thirty years. I couldn't stand the thought of his name being forever stained by a robbery. I hid the money. When nobody came looking for it after a few years, I invested it." She looked at Dane. "I haven't touched a penny of the principal, and only a little of the interest. If you can find whoever it belongs to, I'll gladly return it."

Dane and Stacey stayed that night with her grandmother. When they left the next day to return to Hope Springs, Dane told Gwen not to worry about the money.

"I'll poke around quietly and see what I can find

out,'' he promised, ''but after all this time, it's not likely I'll find anything.''

When they drove away, Stacey hugged Dane's arm. ''Thank you.''

''For what?''

''For easing her mind. That wasn't easy for her.'' She shook her head. ''All my life my family has struggled for money, and she had that all this time, but didn't consider it hers to use.''

''She's a special lady.''

''Yes,'' Stacey agreed. ''She is.''

''So's her granddaughter.''

Stacey smiled. ''Well, now. I think I like the sound of that. Does that mean you're not going to turn tail and leave me at the altar?''

''The day I leave you at the altar is the day that saying on your pajamas comes true.''

## *Epilogue*

Stacey Conner Landers and Wyatt County Sheriff Dane Powell were married two months later. The ceremony was small, but the reception, held in the high school gymnasium at the insistence of the Wilder women—it was the only place in town large enough to accommodate everyone who wanted to congratulate their sheriff—was huge.

The whole county buzzed about the fact that Ace Wilder gave the bride away, and that Jack Wilder stood as Dane's best man. Equally fascinating was that the bride was attended by her grandmother, Gwen Conners of Cheyenne, plus Belinda, Lisa, Laurie and Rachel Wilder.

The story of Stacey's grandfather and their connection to the Wilders, plus the news that Dane was another long-lost son of the late King Wilder, were secrets no longer.

The unexplained twenty thousand dollars, however, remained a private matter. Dane found no report of any large sum of money gone missing back around the time Gwen Conners received the box of cash from Ralph just before he died. As far as Dane was concerned, the money was Gwen's.

At the wedding reception, attended by more than one hundred well-wishers, Ace Wilder held up his cup of punch and called for quiet.

The room gradually hushed until all eyes were centered on him and the newlyweds at his side.

"A toast," Ace said, his deep voice carrying the length of the big room. "To the bride and groom, Stacey and Dane, whom we all welcome into our family with great gladness. As you all know, in 1894 a man named John Wilder, a minor baron over from England on an extended hunting trip, sat down one night in Laramie to a game of cards with a Wyoming rancher named Jeremiah Conner. John Wilder won the final hand that night, and with it, the Conner Ranch, which he renamed the Flying Ace. Now, with the joining of Dane, the great-grandson of John Wilder, and Stacey, the great-great-granddaughter of Jeremiah Conner, the circle is met. The separate sagas of the Wilders and the Conners are now forever joined." He raised his cup high in the air. "Here's to the bride and groom and the future generations."

"Here, here!"

A loud cheer rose from the crowd.

Stacey and Dane tapped their cups against each other's, against Ace's, and everyone around them, then they drank to Ace's toast.

Then, with more than a hundred people looking

on, Dane turned Stacey into his arms and kissed her.
"I love you."

The crowd roared with approval and good wishes.

On the back side of the snack table, with cake
stuck to their faces and fingers, the Wilder children
decided the food was good, but everything else was
just plain dumb.

"Marriage," Jason said with all the disgust of a
nine-year-old. "You won't catch me ever getting
married."

Clay, his seven-year-old brother, clapped him on
the shoulder. "I'm with you, bro."

Behind them, Carrie and Amy, their seven- and
six-year-old cousins-by-marriage, shared equally de-
vious grins. "Wanna bet?" they said.

*  *  *  *  *

Beloved author
# JOAN ELLIOTT PICKART
introduces the next generation of MacAllisters in

*The Baby Bet:*
**MacALLISTER'S GIFTS**

with the following heartwarming romances:

### On sale July 2002

**THE ROYAL MacALLISTER**
Silhouette Special Edition #1477
As the MacAllisters prepare for a royal wedding,
Alice "Trip" MacAllister meets her own Prince Charming.

### On sale September 2002

**PLAIN JANE MacALLISTER**
Silhouette Desire #1462
A secret child stirs up trouble—and long-buried
passions—for Emily MacAllister when she is reunited
with her son's father, Dr. Mark Maxwell.

And look for the next exciting installment of
the MacAllister family saga, coming only to
Silhouette Special Edition in December 2002.

*Don't miss these unforgettable romances…*
*available at your favorite retail outlet.*

*Silhouette* ®
*Where love comes alive* ™

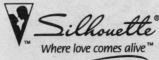

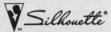

**Where royalty and romance
go hand in hand...**

The series continues in Silhouette Romance
with these unforgettable novels:

**HER ROYAL HUSBAND**
by Cara Colter
on sale July 2002 (SR #1600)

**THE PRINCESS HAS AMNESIA!**
by Patricia Thayer
on sale August 2002 (SR #1606)

**SEARCHING FOR HER PRINCE**
by Karen Rose Smith
on sale September 2002 (SR #1612)

And look for more Crown and Glory stories in
SILHOUETTE DESIRE starting in October 2002!

*Available at your favorite retail outlet.*

*Where love comes alive*™

# Silhouette

# SPECIAL EDITION™
# &
# SILHOUETTE Romance

present a new series about the proud,
passion-driven dynasty

### THE
# COLTONS

**You loved the California Coltons, now discover
the Coltons of Black Arrow, Oklahoma.
Comanche blood courses through their veins,
but a brand-new birthright awaits them....**

WHITE DOVE'S PROMISE by Stella Bagwell (7/02, SE#1478)

THE COYOTE'S CRY by Jackie Merritt (8/02, SE#1484)

WILLOW IN BLOOM by Victoria Pade (9/02, SE#1490)

THE RAVEN'S ASSIGNMENT by Kasey Michaels (9/02, SR#1613)

A COLTON FAMILY CHRISTMAS by Judy Christenberry,
Linda Turner and Carolyn Zane (10/02, Silhouette Single Title)

SKY FULL OF PROMISE by Teresa Southwick (11/02, SR#1624)

THE WOLF'S SURRENDER by Sandra Steffen (12/02, SR#1630)

*Look for these titles
wherever Silhouette books are sold!*

# Silhouette®
*Where love comes alive*™

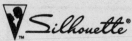

# COMING NEXT MONTH

## SPECIAL EDITION

**#1477 THE ROYAL MacALLISTER—Joan Elliott Pickart**
*The Baby Bet: The MacAllister Family*
Independent-minded Alice "Trip" MacAllister and ravishing royal
Brent Bardow, cousin of the Prince of Wilshire, were unexpectedly in
love. Problem was, a once-burned Brent was wary of women with
"secret agendas." But, when Brent discovered that Alice, too, had her
own agenda, would he flee in anger…or help turn Alice's dreams
into reality?

**#1478 WHITE DOVE'S PROMISE—Stella Bagwell**
*The Coltons: Commanche Blood*
Kerry WindWalker's precious baby girl had gone missing, and
only Jared Colton could save her. The former town bad boy was
proclaimed a hero—but all he wanted as a reward was Kerry. Would
spending time with the beautiful single mom and her adorable tot
transform this rugged rescuer into a committed family man?

**#1479 THE BEST MAN'S PLAN—Gina Wilkins**
It was only make-believe, right? Small-town shopkeeper
Grace Pennington and millionaire businessman Bryan Falcon
were just *pretending* to be in love so the ever-hungry tabloids
would leave Bryan alone. But then the two shared a sizzling night
of passion, and their secret scheme turned into a real-life romance!

**#1480 THE McCAFFERTYS: SLADE—Lisa Jackson**
*The McCaffertys*
Slade McCafferty was the black sheep of his family—and the man
who once shattered lawyer Jamie Parson's young heart. But then
Jamie returned to her hometown for work, and the spark between the
polished attorney and the rugged rogue ignited into fiery desire.
Would a shocking injury resolve past hurts…and make way for a
heartfelt declaration?

**#1481 MAD ENOUGH TO MARRY—Christie Ridgway**
*Stood up…on prom night!* Elena O'Brien, who grew up on the wrong
side of the tracks, had never forgotten—or forgiven—rich boy Logan
Chase. Eleven years later, Elena wound up living under one roof with
Logan, and new desires began to simmer. Then another prom night
arrived, and Logan finally had a chance to
prove his true love for his old flame….

**#1482 HIS PRIVATE NURSE—Arlene James**
A suspicious fall had landed sexy Royce Lawler in the hospital and in
the care of pretty nurse Merrily Gage. And when it was time to go
home Royce offered Merrily the position of his private nurse—a job
she happily accepted, never realizing that caring for her handsome
patient would throw both her heart and her life in danger.